FIRST CLASS

Fling

KAYLENE WINTER

Chapter One

I'M BURNED OUT.

A woman with charred edges, a hollow center, and so bone tired no amount of sleep will ever make a difference.

It's the price I pay for perfect service, glowing reviews, and a restaurant people whisper about as the future of Spanish dining in the Pacific Northwest.

Sadly, I can't remember the last time I enjoyed a meal without reducing it to numbers on a spreadsheet.

All of it's been worth it, I think. Hard work has played a huge part in rebuilding my family's legacy.

Delgado Cocina Española started as my father's dream thirty years ago. A kitschy Spanish-themed diner complete with flamenco posters on the walls, paella drowning in saffron, and laminated menus curling at the corners. The restaurant was our entire family life. My brother, sister, and I worked alongside my parents from the time I could walk.

I loved it. Something was missing.

At eighteen I bolted to find my roots. First in Madrid then Seville and finally Barcelona, where, for three years, I learned how to cook from some of the finest chefs in the world.

I survived kitchens designed to break me and came home with scars, burns, skill, and a hunger to tear the old place down to its bones.

It took some convincing, but my parents believed in my vision and we gutted it. Modernized the space into a fine-dining establishment complete with season-driven menus and wine lists celebrating Spain using ingredients from the Pacific Northwest.

Now critics come from around the world. Foodies beg for reservations. My father, who should have retired years ago, still takes care of the customers while I oversee the rest of the details from top to bottom.

Ten years later, and I don't know which end is up.

Somehow, my family noticed. My mom and dad conspired with Marcella, my older sister, lawyer, best friend, and eternal thorn. The three of them staged a kitchen ambush last week, blocking the walk-in door until I promised not only to take a vacation, but to stay out of the restaurant for an *entire month*.

Which is how I ended up here at SeaTac, boarding a flight to Barcelona clutching a ticket reading Seat 2C.

The first-class cabin glows with gold light, a cathedral of quiet wealth. Suites are arranged 1–2–1. One by each window, two in the center, another single across. I slide into the center seat. The soft, buttery leather hugs me in a way the booths back home never do.

A flute of champagne appears before I can protest. I take a sip. Dry, tart, faintly apple. I set it down fast, scared I'll start to enjoy myself and then realize, I'm *supposed* to be having fun.

I take another swig as my phone buzzes three times in succession.

Marcella: No emails. Your job is
to sleep, eat and hopefully find
someone to tickle your kitty.

Mamà: Have fun! We love you.

Papà: Don't worry about anything.
Enjoy your time away!

God love the three of them. They're annoying as fuck but their hearts are in the right place. I switch my phone off. If they want me to relax, I'm gonna start now by ghosting them for doing this to me.

The overhead clicks shut across from me, causing me to glance over.

A man slides into 2D next to me.

Time slows, rewinds, rearranges. He's tall, six feet at least. Long lines and controlled movement. Olive skin. Dark-brown hair, white shirt unbuttoned at the throat. Sleeves rolled, revealing forearms meant for both tasting and teasing.

My breath catches unexpectedly. I have to shift in my seat because my pussy pulses and my panties become damp.

No.

Not happening. This trip isn't about men. My history proves I pick disasters. Line cooks who drink through prep. Food vendors who sob like babies when I'm too busy to spend time with them. Bartenders who kiss and steal in the same breath.

I glance at my reflection in the black screen across from me. In the real world, I have no apron to hide behind. My wardrobe is abysmal. Today I'm wearing worn black jeans, a fitted tank under a hoodie and plain boots. My hair is twisted into a high knot, held together by a giant hair claw. Without any makeup, freckles are visible across my cheeks.

I'm not glamorous. Certainly not first-class sleek. Especially next to this guy. He exudes expensive. Women probably trip over themselves for a smile I haven't seen yet.

In any case, it's obvious he belongs up here in the bougie seats, not me.

I try not to stare as he settles in without fuss, like the world makes space for him. He smells faintly of cedar and fresh air.

The divider between our seats sits half-raised, a beige suggestion of privacy.

I could lift it. I don't.

He doesn't either.

The plane pushes back. Engines growl, the cabin angles up, and we lift into the night.

To keep my mind off my handsome neighbor, I pick up the glossy, bound menu to peruse. The pages promise gourmet offerings like salmon blini, beef tenderloin, seared cod, pavlova. Fancy food designed to seduce passengers into forgetting they're eating reheats at thirty thousand feet.

I can't help but smirk. My chef brain hungers for something else. Barcelona tapas, savory paella, seafood markets. The things I should have researched, planned, anticipated. I didn't have the bandwidth. By the time Marcella forced this ticket down my throat, I was too fried to arrange anything.

So here I am, a chef without a plan, hungry without knowing what for.

The attendant returns. "Ms. Delgado?"

"Cod. Pavlova. Albariño." I decide on the fly.

She turns to him.

His voice pours low, Rioja-rich. "The same."

Good God. The accent. My nipples throb. My pussy clenches again, sharp and insistent.

I stare straight ahead, heat flushing my skin.

Silence stretches. Not awkward, charged. At least for me. Every nerve is attuned to him. The warmth radiating from his body. The faint scrape of his watch on the leather armrest. Even the rhythm of his breath.

I find myself imagining him leaning closer. His lips brush my ear as his hand slides over mine. He presses me back into this wide leather seat, parting my legs under the blanket. Sinks his manicured fingers into my pussy until I'm writhing at thirty thousand feet.

The visual slams through me so hard I gasp.

Mortified, I grab my champagne and drain what's left. My cheeks blaze. If he looked at me now, he'd *know*.

Crossing my legs tight, I force my gaze to the screen in front of me where the tiny airplane charts our journey.

"You vacationing in Barcelona?" The man's accent cradles each word.

I peer over. "Yes."

"Ahh. My home. In Barcelona, mornings don't rush you. They unfold leisurely, like something waiting to be savored."

Jesus.

Heat shoots through me, even though his description is a bit cheesy. He doesn't know me, can't—but with two sentences he's named the city as I remember it. Butter bleeding from fresh pastry, shutters banging, oranges stacked like suns in wooden crates.

Of course, he could mean something entirely different...

"So true." I swallow, pushing the thought out of my mind. "I studied there."

His mouth curves, one corner only, a smile built for secrets. "Then you understand."

Oh, I do. Too much. My body is still whirring from the fantasy I didn't mean to conjure. His hand under my blanket, spreading me and stroking my clit until I beg for him to make me come in gasps.

My heart pounds low and hot. My panties are soaked.

It's absurd. I don't know his name. He could be married. He could be the kind of man who flirts with women on every flight and forgets them before landing.

Beside him, I feel like a waif. Not glamorous. Not polished. Certainly not the kind of woman men like him notice.

Still, I can't deny how turned on I am. Proof my body has already betrayed me.

Maybe Marcella was correct. I should open myself up. She took a chance and is now married to a gorgeous doctor who's eight years younger than her. I grip the armrest, desperate to anchor myself.

Coming back to reality, who am I kidding? This guy is a stranger on a plane. I have too much responsibility. I can't afford to make any mistakes. I'm spending my time in Spain eating and drinking. Research.

The smart move is obvious. Pull out my headphones, close the divider, throw on a movie and crash until we land.

Keep this man a beautiful question mark I never try to answer.

Except...it's hard to ignore the buzz in my body and the ache for more than food or sleep. I'd be lying if I denied the way my heart yearns for someone beside me and how my soul whispers about a family I've never dared to imagine.

I shut my eyes, draw in a breath, and remind myself silence is safe.

The truth presses hard in my ribs.

I don't want safe. I want to fall into the abyss.

The question is, am I brave enough?

Chapter Two

I RECOGNIZE HER THE moment I sit down.

Not from photographs. Or puff pieces in travel magazines. We've never actually met, after all.

I know of Rosa Delgado because she fascinates me.

I've eaten at Delgado Cocina Española a few times. Never as Santiago Rivas, Master Sommelier. I dine the way some people go to church. Quiet, humbled, aching to *feel* something.

And I do. Oh, how I do.

Word of Rosa Delgado and her family restaurant reached me fast when it first opened. A native Spaniard doesn't ignore it when the industry whispers of a woman cooking Spanish food better than most kitchens in Madrid. In Tacoma, no less.

I couldn't stay away.

It wasn't long before critics were clamoring to praise her. The past couple years, the powers that be are talking James Beard, and they're right. Her food isn't loud. It's exact.

The lamb with Montsant still lives on my tongue, tannins cutting through fat before yielding to smoke. Her anchovy with Albariño has a purity so sharp I quoted it to a room of young sommeliers in Lyon. They scribbled notes as if I'd given them gospel.

Of course, she never noticed me. Or knew how much I admired her.. Rosa Delgado has no idea who I am.

Now she's beside me on the way to Barcelona. My seatmate. What amazing luck.

Before now, I've only seen her in a chef coat with her hair under a scarf. Tonight, she looks no older than twenty. Curled under a blanket in comfortable clothing. Freckles scattered across her cheeks. Lips plush even when pressed tight. Not glamorous by any stretch, but stunning, nonetheless.

In her kitchen she commands with steel. Here she shrinks, almost as if she's shy.

The contradiction fascinates me.

The attendant appears. "Ms. Delgado?"

"Cod. Pavlova. Albariño." Rosa's voice is calm, but I notice her fingers tighten on the edge of the blanket.

"The same." I place my menu in the side pocket of my seat.

On the surface, it's professional reflex. I've trusted her palate before, quoting her pairings to students as examples of fearless precision. Following her lead is a no-brainer. Even though its airplane food, what a cool opportunity for me to get her take on things.

When the attendant moves on, I catch Rosa's profile. Eyes shadowed, lashes low. Awareness prickles across my skin.

"You vacationing in Barcelona" I make an attempt to soften the edges of my accent

She glances over, almost surprised to hear me address her. "Yes."

"My home. Barcelona doesn't wake in a rush. Mornings open slowly, like something meant to be savored." I manage to stop myself from wincing. I didn't mean for my words to come out like a pick-up line.

Luckily, she doesn't seem to notice my faux pas.

By the look in her eyes, I bet she's thinking about La Boqueria before tourists crowd its aisles. I picture her wandering through the market where scallops glint like half moons. *Jamón ibérico* hangs overhead, fat shining under pale light. Citrus lines up beside stacks of thick tomatoes. Copper pans clang in the small bars tucked between stalls. Everywhere, voices are low with anticipation of whatever treasure they've purchased.

"So true." She fidgets with the hem of the blanket. "I studied there."

Her gaze drops, as if she's said too much, though she hasn't uttered more than a few words. For the tiniest moment, I glimpse a woman who'd rather hide than be seen.

Still, I've opened the door and I don't want it to close. Her opinions are a treasure. I want to hear her voice again, even if she guards herself carefully.

I could tell her I know her work, I've been to her restaurant and tasted her food. Spoken her name to my students. It's too early, though, and my instinct tells me timing matters.

I won't overwhelm or expose her, she's minding her own business, after all. When we speak, I want her curious, not cornered.

Frankly, it surprises me how much I care. As a frequent flyer, most conversations are usually disposable. Weather. Professions. Fun facts about whatever the destination is. Polite noise forgotten before landing.

With Rosa Delgado beside me, I don't want disposable. I want a thread strong enough to carry us through these hours in the air. Maybe even further. Letting this opportunity slip away s unthinkable.

I keep it simple. "Then you understand."

Before she can reply, the food arrives. She takes a few polite bites, then sets her fork down. No grimace, no complaint, but the absence of pleasure is clear.

Rosa Delgado isn't the type to fake delight. I admire her conviction.

"In Barcelona," I lean toward her, "I always start at the markets. Taste what's fresh, see what calls loudest."

Her eyes flick to mine, curiosity edging past her guard. "La Boqueria is my favorite market in the world."

Aha. Nailed it.

I nod. "Mine too. You can eat better at one of those counters than at half the fine-dining rooms in the city."

"I miss eating food I didn't make myself." She gazes into the distance as if this is a revelation.

"Hmmm." Her admission settles between us. "So you cook?"

A pause. Then, with a small lift of her chin, "I'm a chef."

I let her claim the word. I don't press, don't mention I already know.

Not yet.

"And when you last ate someone else's cuisine?" I probe.

She exhales, eyes lowering. "Every bite felt like a gift."

"I hope Barcelona blesses you with many gifts." I beam at her.

Her mouth twitches into almost a smile. Enough to undo me.

I lean closer. "I should introduce myself. Santiago Rivas. I cofounded Viñedo Hospitality Group, we oversee wine programs for properties across the U.S. and Europe. I spend more time in cellars and airports than at home."

"Intriguing. What were you doing in Seattle" Her eyes widen. "By the way, I'm Rosa."

I decide to toe my way in. "'I have a small condo here, though sadly work hasn't allowed me to spend much time in the area yet. Now that I've met you, perhaps I'll make more effort."

Color blooms across her cheeks. She lowers her chin, self-consciously.

"I didn't mean to make you uncomfortable, Rosa. All I meant was it's very nice to meet you." I shift gears.

"Uh, you didn't, exactly. I'm a bit out of my element when I'm not working." She glances away, gripping the blanket like I'm going to rip it off her.

God, I want to. She's exquisite.

Desire surges through me. My cock thickens, tenting the wool of my pants as I imagine her lips wrapped around me, cheeks hollowing, tongue sliding along the sensitive vein under my crown. I imagine her pussy wet and open, my fingers buried. Her hips rocking until she gasps my name.

Jesus. I've got to retain some control. I grip the armrest, inhale, exhale. I'm not a man for one-night stands. They've always been hollow. I'm not great at relationships, either. I lost my marriage to airports, hotels, and empty beds.

It's been so long and, admittedly, I want connection. Rosa Delgado, curling into herself beside me, makes me ache for it.

"How long will you be there?" I manage to say.

She frowns. "An entire month."

"Me too. Should be more than enough time for you to remember how to taste." My voice sounds gravelly. Pained.

This time, her breath falters. She catches the double edge, and I see the spark of interest before she looks down. My gut confirms she's introverted not standoff-ish. Careful, but not closed.

The plates are taken away and the cabin dims. Rosa pulls the blanket tighter, trying to fold smaller. I want to tell her to stretch, to take space, to sprawl. Instead, I push the divider down all the way, lean close, and speak softly in a pitch for her alone to hear.

"If you want silence, I'm good at silence. If you want company, I'm good at conversation too."

Her gaze snaps to mine, startled. Heat there, no denying.

Hope, maybe.

I sit back, though every muscle in me fights the distance. My cock still throbs at the images in my mind. Rosa straddling me in this wide leather seat, pussy sliding down onto me slow and wet while the cabin sleeps. I'd keep Rosa steady on my lap until her lip caught between her teeth. Her body trembling as she tries to keep her cries quiet. The man across the aisle stirring in his sleep, unaware of our paradise inches away.

My pulse hammers but I manage to calm myself down. Now isn't the time.

Barcelona waits. Markets at dawn. Wine she didn't pour. Meals she didn't labor over. Mornings she hasn't allowed herself in years.

Maybe fate put her here, beside me, to remind her she doesn't have to do everything alone. Maybe, for once, I'm meant to be the one who looks after her.

Rosa's eyes shift toward me, hesitation laced with curiosity. *Interest.* I sense the question building on her tongue, the urge to close the silence between us.

Somehow, I keep control.

Hold still. Remain steady.

Giving her the space to choose.

Chapter Three

My heart's beating so fast I can barely catch my breath.

Santiago's words linger between us: *If you want silence, I'm good at silence. If you want company, I'm good at conversation too.*

Something in the way he said it makes me comfortable. He isn't pushing. He's offering.

My whole life runs on demands, commands, expectations. A subtle invitation is...rare.

"I'll take the company."

His mouth curves, not a smirk, or polished charm. Steady. Happy.

It unnerves me more than a perfect, toothy grin ever could.

Around us, strangers settle in for the night, burrowing under blankets flicking through which movie they'll fall asleep to. The two of us recline our seats to flat and turn toward each other.

The world narrows to the two of us in our wide, plush seats and a single conversation.

I tip my chin toward him. "So. Viñedo Hospitality. You cofounded it?"

He nods, fingers resting loose on the armrest. "In New York. A few of us believed we could build wine programs better than what we saw. We blinked and two decades later, we realized we were international." A dry smile. "Growth was relentless. I lived in airports. Slept in cellars. My marriage ended somewhere in the middle."

His bluntness makes me blink. Most men coat their romantic history in lacquer. Or, blame the woman. He sets his down raw, owning his part.

"Do you miss her?" The words slip out before I can stop them.

His pause is brief, but real. "I miss what we could have been if I'd learned how to balance my life more."

The honesty cuts sharper than the confession itself. "I get it. Delgado Cocina nearly broke me before it saved me. My father's place was great, but outdated. I stripped it to the bones and convinced him to let me build something new. Everyone thought I'd lost my mind. Now we're successful and my folks are essentially retired. Most nights? I collapse alone."

"Do you regret it?" His eyes bore into mine

I breathe out slowly. "Some days. Not always. I love it. I hate it. It's mine."

"Yes." He nods once, certain. "The only way anything worth keeping is built."

The words land, loosening something in me I didn't realize had been locked. "Before New York? Where did you learn wine?"

"La Rioja." His expression shifts, softer. "My father's family vineyard. I spent every summer sticky with grape juice. Winters were freezing cold in the cellars. I left at eighteen. First Barcelona. Then Bordeaux. Even though they sold it long ago, the smell of fermenting grapes clings to me. Sometimes I think it lives in my skin."

The picture he paints hits me full in the chest. I envision a young Santiago, dark hair tangled, running through rows of vines, soles dusted, palms stained purple. A man carved by earth before elegance touched him.

"Wow. It sounds…" I search. *"Alive."*

His smile is coy. "And you? Where did you first learn to love food?"

"In my parents' kitchen. My mother's hands buried in dough, my father hovering over paella. My sister, Marcella sneaking olives like it was a sport. Food was the language we all understood."

"Better than boys?" His tone teases me, but the question sits heavier underneath, considering my abysmal track record.

"Much better." My laugh comes sharp, surprising me. "Food doesn't cheat. Or ghost. Or drink too much. I seem to collect men who need saving."

"Do you want to fix them?" He quirks a brow.

"I guess I *did.*" I stiffen because it's hard to admit. "So stupid. I've been burned, for sure. Fire can look beautiful until it leaves scars, right?"

Santiago doesn't flinch or fill the quiet with comfort. He lets my confession breathe for a bit before he replies. "Maybe you should try someone who doesn't want or need saving."

The air between us changes. Is he hitting on me? It's been so long, I've lost the ability to tell. My pulse jumps like a warning I don't want to heed.

"And you?" I'm compelled to redirect to his personal life since I confessed so much of mine. "Have you dated much after your marriage broke up?"

"No." His reply comes without hesitation. "One-night stands leave me hollow. Relationships? I failed at the one that mattered. It's hard to believe I'd ever be successful again, given my current schedule."

Huh. So, he's *not* hitting on me. Or, if he is, this is a fling situation. Which means he's probably a no-go for me.

Not probably. *Definitely*.

Thankfully, the flight attendants arrive with bedding so we can settle into our makeshift beds. Once we're reclined side-by-side, the romantic confessions are put to the side and we seamlessly shift into a more neutral, yet lively discussion about our love of food and wine.

When I admit I can't stand over-oaked Chardonnay, he clutches his chest like I've wounded him mortally. We cover our favorite cities, food, travel. He needles me about Tacoma, I jab at his sommelier pretension. He's witty, goofy and self-depreciating. When he describes teaching wine seminars in Lyon, he exaggerates his students' awe until I'm laughing so hard I have to cover my mouth to avoid annoying the rest of the first-class cabin.

It's a moment before I realize the sound of my own laugher has startled me. I can't remember the last time utter joy bubbled up unplanned before I could smother it.

I shake my head, grinning despite myself. "I've never spoken this much to a stranger."

"You don't seem like a stranger." His smile is genuine, almost like it's meant for me.

His words slip under my skin, leaving me breathless.

I should rebuild the wall, put space back between us. Instead, I lean closer, reckless. "Me either."

As we lie side by side facing each other, I have no idea how much time has passed. Except for our quiet conversation and the faint thrum of engines, the cabin is quiet. Around us, people sleep, oblivious to the fact my world has folded to fit inside two lie-flat leather seats in the first-class cabin.

Dangerous.

Subtly, I study him. Santiago has broad shoulders and elegant hands. His dark hair falls perfectly out of place and his eyes remain steady on me like I'm worth the attention. He's present. Attentive. Interested in me.

"You know," I whisper. "Based on first impressions, I thought you'd be different."

He rests his head on his hand. "Different how?"

"When you sat down, I pegged you for a player. You come across so polished. I figured you'd be the kind of guy who seduces with vintages and perfect pours."

"And now?"

I bite my lip. "Your life is actually fascinating. Enviable. Best of all, when it comes to food and wine, you're nerdy like me. In a delightful way."

His laugh is gleeful, genuine. "*Nerdy?*"

"When we first started talking, I thought you were going to sell me a tour or something."

He groans, rubbing his forehead, but he's smiling. "Failure."

"Oh, you redeemed yourself." I can't help stop the words from slipping out. It's my Achilles heel. I'm honest as a cut.

His smile fades into something deeper, slower. He doesn't move, doesn't crowd me. He just looks at me. Waits.

I should stop here. Instead, curiosity overwhelms me. "For someone so worldly, how did you end up with a condo in Seattle?"

A flicker of something crosses his face. "When I left New York after my divorce, I needed a drastic change. Seattle is close enough to Europe, far enough from the noise. And the rain... I actually love. It slows you down whether you want it to or not."

I hear the truth underneath. He's a man who needed saving from his own momentum.

We have this in common.

For the first time in my life, I have instant connection.

Damn it, I don't want this night to ever end.

I tip my head, steady and strong. "Tell me how..."

Chapter Four

WHEN I SAT NEXT to Rosa Delgado, the chef whose food had lingered on my tongue longer than most memories, I'd imagined polite talk about flavor profiles and sourcing.

Safe conversation two professionals might have on a long flight.

Nothing more.

Instead, I find myself discussing things I've never talked about with anyone. Not even my own family.

"When I left New York after my divorce, I needed a drastic change," I admit. "Seattle is close enough to Europe, far enough from the noise. And the rain... I actually love. It slows you down whether you want it to or not."

The words are strange on my tongue. Soft, unguarded. The thing is, it wasn't a marriage ending. It was war. Lawyers. Settlements. Years of building a business from nothing, only to watch half of it torn away. My name scraped off the door, clients siphoned, reputation bruised.

Starting over nearly broke me.

But here, beside Rosa, the ache turns quiet. Old resentments and fear recede, leaving a sense of peace I can't explain. Like, maybe it all led me here. To this moment.

She doesn't press. She doesn't need to. Her eyes hold the same exhaustion I've carried for years. The kind ambition hides until it burns through every ounce of calm you have left.

For the first time in years, my heart is light.

I can't name what this is. Connection? Recognition? Fate? All I know is it moves through me, steady as the engines beneath our feet.

Damn it, I don't want this night to end.

She tips her head, eyes fixed on mine. "Tell me how…"

So I do. Slowly at first, then all at once. I tell her how Viñedo rose from the ashes of what I lost. How I rebuilt everything with steadier hands, fewer illusions, more scars. She listens without interrupting, tracing the rim of her glass as if it keeps her tethered to my voice.

I speak about my brother in Barcelona, though not specifically about the deal waiting there. I'm too superstitious.

For the first time, however, I admit aloud how tired I am of chasing success. How focusing only on business leaves me lonely.

Her gaze never drifts. She listens like no one ever has. Like every word matters.

Somewhere mid-story, her eyes grow heavy, blinking slower with each breath. She fights it by asking questions. Small, probing, thoughtful things. But, her voice fades softer each time.

When her lashes lower for the third time, I know the battle's lost.

Her eyes flutter closed midsentence, then snap open again.

I can't ignore the fatigue dragging her down. It lives in her posture, even when she's lying down. Her voice is hoarse. Gravelly.

She's fought exhaustion throughout our delightful conversation because she's built for endurance.

As disappointed as I am, even steel bends.

"You should rest." I reach over and tuck her hair behind her ear.

She shakes her head, stubborn, though the corners of her mouth betray her with a tired slant. "I'm fine."

"Rosa," I soothe. "*Sleep*. There's always tomorrow."

She exhales, long and low, and lets the fight slip from her body.

I lean in and press my lips to her forehead.

Her lashes flutter once. Then she sinks, steady breathing pulling her under.

A quiet protectiveness threads through me.

Her body softens into the seat, tension unwinding at last. The strand of dark hair slips free again, catching the light from the aisle. Her lips part with each breath. A faint sound escapes, something between a sigh and surrender. The pulse at her throat beats slow, steady, alive.

She looks younger like this. Not in years, but in consequence. The exhaustion she wears like armor slides off her shoulders, leaving only peace. I want to keep her in this safe space, untouched by noise, obligation, or anything draining her brilliance.

"I've wanted to meet you for a long time," I whisper. "You've surprised me more than I imagined."

For years, I've been surrounded by people, but alone. This is different. I can't wait until she wakes up so we can talk again.

The cabin vibrates with white noise. I let my head fall back, though my eyes refuse to close.

Barcelona waits. For once, I don't think of it as a destination for meetings and cellars. I picture places I want her to see. Not the usual pilgrimage spots. She deserves better.

I visualize us strolling the cloisters of the Pedralbes Monastery, where silence is cloaked in velvet and light breaks through gothic arches. Or the hills above the city, Tibidabo rising with its strange mix of church and amusement park. Not glamorous, but honest. We'd stand at the rail with Barcelona spread beneath us, red roofs tumbling toward the sea. In Gràcia, small plazas would claim her heart. The kind where old men sip vermut while children chase soccer balls.

Rosa doesn't need Michelin stars, she needs a clay dish of bombas. Garlic still hot in oil. Laughter filling the square.

Maybe I could take her farther to the fishing village of Cadaqués, whitewashed above the sea, salt crusting the air. Or inland, to Rioja, where vines claw into slate and the wines taste like the earth itself refused to give up. Perhaps I could show her my family's old vineyard...

All these places flash through me, but what stays is the image of her smiling.

Rosa, unburdened.

Rosa, fed without lifting a pan.

Rosa, definitively cared for.

I've never let myself imagine a future with someone this soon. With other women, desire has been singular. Usually just sex. A temporary high of connection.

I want Rosa, of course. God. My cock has been hard all night. But, my stronger urge is to protect her. Give her a safe space where she can enjoy life and doesn't need to prove herself.

Her hand shifts in sleep, fingers curling toward the edge of my seat. I almost cover them with mine, but stop.

She deserves rest without interruption.

So, I close my eyes at last, surrendering to the rhythm of her breaths, the steady thrum of engines, the pull of possibility.

Barcelona waits.

For the first time in years, I look forward to something more than work when we land.

Chapter Five

THE CAPTAIN'S VOICE SLICES through me. "Ladies and gentlemen, we'll begin our descent into Barcelona shortly."

My eyes fly open. Neck kinked, mouth dry, blanket twisted around my waist. For a breath I don't know where I am. Then the cabin sharpens: low light, the faint hiss of vents, a row of screens gone black.

Santiago's seat is mostly upright. His eyes are half-lidded and the man's hair is rumpled in a way no grooming product could fake.

Memory rolls back slow and thick. His voice in the dark hours. Viñedo rising from wreckage. Rain in Seattle slowing a man who didn't know how to stop. An intimate conversation usually saved for trusted friends.

Somehow he gave it to me.

Heat climbs my cheeks when I remember: I fell asleep while he was in the middle of a story.

I thumb the seat controls. The back slides up with a soft whir. My reflection glares from the dead screen in front of me. Wild hair. Mascara smudges. Not to mention, poo breath.

A glamorous morning, Delgado. *Perfect.*

"Buenos días." His words are soft, sanded by sleep.

"Morning." I rake fingers through my hair, trying to tame the chaos. "Please tell me I didn't snore."

He smiles without answering my question and I notice the lines crinkle at the corners of his eyes. "You drifted off quickly. I took it as a compliment."

My cheeks heat. "Passing out during your life story is a *compliment?*"

"Of course." He leans toward me. "You trusted me enough to finally get some rest."

I have no words. Santiago is perfection. Too wonderful to be true.

The world around us comes into focus, unfortunately. The cabin brightens as window shades lift. A flight attendant glides past with a cart, her ponytail sharp enough to cut glass. Coffee steams in paper cups. Small white trays land on our tables—eggs, a grilled tomato slice, fruit arranged in an unnatural rainbow, a croissant so symmetrical it looks 3D printed.

I stare down, appetite flatlining. The eggs are unappetizing. The croissant's layers read like plastic. My stomach tightens in revolt.

"You're not eating?" He quirks a brow.

"I can't." I nudge the tray away with one finger. "Not when I can grab breakfast in town later."

He lifts his fork, anyway, cuts a neat bite. "Travel has trained me to accept a placeholder. Real meals happen after wheels touch down."

"I vote real meal." I inch my coffee toward me. It's thin and bitter but still warm enough to anchor me. I take a sip and glance past the aisle, where light spills through another passenger's window. Dawn filters across the cabin in soft gold streaks.

Even without seeing the city, I can feel it. Barcelona waking somewhere below. It tugs at something deep inside me.

"You look like you're already out there."

"Maybe I am." I glance back at him.

He studies my face like it's a map. Says nothing, yet somehow I know he understands.

With breakfast cleared away, overhead bins thud open. Seatbelts click. Noise replaces hush. Passengers around us prepare for landing and the night we shared folds itself tight, tucked into a place where I keep impossible things.

I'm sad, I realize. I don't connect with people often. Especially men. I wish I'd made more effort to stay awake.

"Did I really poop out last night?" I lean toward him. "Before you were finished?"

"It's okay." There is no judgment in his words.

Guilt loosens its hold, replaced by a warmer ache of the probability I'll never see Santiago again. I rest a palm over the blanket, smoothing a nonexistent crease.

"Where are you staying?" He lowers his voice so I can hear him.

"El Born." I swallow. "From the pictures, it's a quaint little apartment above a shop. Narrow stairs, old tiles. Close to the Gothic Quarter."

The corners of his mouth lift. "Good choice."

"Why?"

"It suits you. No pretense. Practical. Slightly unpredictable." His boyish grin makes me swoon a bit.

Another chime. The seatbelt light pops on. The plane veers to the left. My fingers clamp around the armrest on instinct. I haven't been on an adventure like this since culinary school.

"You'll be fine." He leans in another inch, enough to steady my heart.

I let out air I didn't know I was holding. "Confident, aren't you?"

"About some things."

"Oh?"

"I believe the best things are worth the wait." His reply lands between us, soft as cotton.

Heavy as iron.

Wheels extend. The plane groans. Barcelona spreads beneath us. I picture a geometry of red roofs and crooked streets.

Santiago's hand is millimeters from mine, but he doesn't reach for me. Our eyes are locked on each other, connecting us more intimately than a touch.

Tires kiss the runway with a breathy shudder. As we pull into the gate, the usual chorus begins: zippers, texts, grievances, foreign languages colliding in one echoing hall of human impatience.

We unbuckle. He slips into his jacket gracefully as I anxiously gather my tote, tuck my phone into the side pocket of my backpack, and pat the passport I checked three times already.

We stand when our row empties into the aisle. Shoulder to shoulder in a human river with no patience. He turns, speaks low enough so the words skim my skin.

"Rosa."

I look up.

"There's a small place in El Born." His mouth curves into a quirk. "Can Cisa. It's a quaint wine bar with delicious bites. Meet me there, Wednesday night."

Breath sticks halfway to my lungs. Not an assumption. Not an order.

An opening.

"You're inviting me on a date?"

"If you're up for it. Good wine. Conversation we didn't finish."

I search his face for performance, find none. Only calm certainty, not entitlement.

"Two nights from now," I state the obvious.

"Yes. Two nights." He echoes it like a promise. "My business should be concluded by then."

We move again. The line funnels toward the jet bridge. At the top of the ramp he steps aside, lets me pass. His hand hovers near my back. Not touching. Warm all the same.

"Welcome back," he gestures.

Two words, and the hall expands, then narrows to a single point dead center in my chest.

"I'd walk with you," he explains as we step inside the airport, "but I have to dash. My flat's not far, and I've got a meeting across town. If I don't shower and change first, they may not want to be in a room with me."

A small laugh escapes me. "Go, then. I'll be fine. I wouldn't want to ruin your schedule."

"Rosa," he chuckles. "You couldn't ruin anything."

He steps back to let another passenger pass, eyes lingering on mine for one last beat. "Wednesday," he reminds me. "Can Cisa."

"Wednesday," I echo.

And then, he's gone.

The airport swallows me. Fluorescent glare, polished floors, a river of people dragging their lives behind them on four wheels. Spanish spills over English, Catalan threads between both. Signs point in every direction at once.

I follow the stream toward passport control. The line snakes under an oversize photograph of a beach. Inching forward, I study the faces around me. I'm oddly invisible here on my own. The immigration officer barely glances up before thumping a stamp on my passport.

Baggage claim blooms into a mishmash of carousels. Belts clank to life. Screens flash flight numbers in bold blue. A toddler wails. A woman argues with no one, or everyone, about a missing bag.

As I wait for my suitcase, my phone buzzes with messages in the family text sent during the flight.

```
Mamí: Mija, send a text when you
land. Eat. Sleep. No work.
```

Marcella: Did you meet a poet
on the plane yet? If he quotes
Neruda, run.

Papá: Find the good anchovies.
Bring home.

I smile without meaning to. Type quick answers.

Me: Safe. Will sleep. No poets
yet. Anchovies noted.

Three dots blink, then vanish, then blink again.

Marcella: Proud of you. Remember
fun is not illegal.

I tuck the phone away. The belt coughs up a stream of luggage. All the bags look like mine. Black, black, navy, a neon monstrosity with flamingos, another black. I lose track, snap back, stare harder. My eyes burn. My feet ache inside boots I wore for competence, not airport sprints.

Santiago's words replay on a loop I didn't authorize. Two nights. Can Cisa.

My case rolls by, half-hidden under a duffel. I lunge, grab the handle, wrestle the weight onto the ground with a grunt earning sympathy from a stranger. Once I clear customs, I wheel my bag toward the taxi stand in the cool morning, my hair lifting in a flirt of wind.

While I wait in line, I open maps on my phone. Type Can Cisa. A red pin blossoms and there it is…two doors from my rental.

A sign?

My laugh startles me. A single, disbelieving sound, quickly swallowed by the hustle and bustle of passengers trying to get to their destinations. Coincidence, I tell myself. Barcelona is dense. Streets knot together like veins. Proximity is relative on a phone map, the place could be farther than it looks.

Except none of this seems random. The universe is giggling at me and saying, *"Rosa, go live your life for fuck's sake."*

A taxi idles in front of me. The driver leans across the seat, flips a hand toward the trunk. *"¿Dónde, guapa?"*

"El Born, por favor." I give the street, the number, the landmarks locals use. He nods, pulls into the stream.

Concrete ramps give way to a sliver of highway. Industrial buildings blur into billboards, then flats with laundry strung from narrow balconies like prayers. Graffiti rises and falls in bright bursts. A man on a scooter weaves between lanes. The city unfurls ribbon by ribbon.

Breath loosens inside my ribs.

The driver whistles along to a song on the radio I don't recognize. We slide into streets so narrow I'm afraid the buildings will swipe the sides of the car. The taxi turns twice, then once more, then stops. The building wears its years with a kind of swagger. A wooden door dark with history, carved stone lintel frowning over a knocker shaped like a lion's mouth.

I pay, tip too much, haul my case from the trunk. The driver points up with his chin, a universal gesture I assume means *"Good luck with those stairs, I'm not hauling your bag up there."* I grin, because yes, those stairs look like a dare.

One flight at a time. Colorful green and yellow tiles underfoot. A landing with a cracked mirror framed in gilt. Another flight. A window exposing a slice of sky so blue it borders on absurd. At the top, my rental. A room with tall windows and a view of a street already teeming with life.

From my window I spot a barista pulling shots across the way, a cyclist balancing a crate of oranges, and a woman shaking out a tablecloth from a balcony so close I could catch it.

Then I look left. There, within spitting distance, is a pale-green facade with black letters I know now without needing to look: Can Cisa.

I can't help it. I laugh again, softer this time, a private sound loosening the knot in my chest by another millimeter.

I open my phone. My thumb hovers over messages I could send. Instead, I cross the room, unzip my case, pull out the worn T-shirt I sleep in when no one sees me. I toss it on the bed, then stop.

If I close my eyes, I can conjure up the heat of his hand hovering near my back at the jet bridge. Hear the low promise of meeting again. Feel the light press of his lips as I drifted off to sleep on the plane.

Two nights.

I swallow a grin I don't know how to wear yet.

"Okay," I tell the window. "I'm here. I'm gonna sleep until I wake up, for once."

When I manage to crawl beneath the soft cotton sheets, the room smells of soap and orange peel left in a bowl by the sink. Exhaustion edges in. I don't fight it.

Right before I go under, I picture a pale-green door, a narrow bar crowded with bottles. Wine poured with care, not performance.

A handsome man waits for me.

My mouth curves before I can stop it.

Two nights.

I can't wait.

Chapter Six

The Next Morning

I WAKE BEFORE DAWN.

Anticipation thrums through my entire being.

Lying still, I listen to Barcelona stir below and a vision of her arrives in the quiet.

Rosa.

Not a dream, not memory. A presence.

Her voice threads through the dark like low music. I can hear it. I see her lips part, revealing perfectly white teeth when she smiled on the plane. The flush climbing her throat when she spoke about needing rest. The way her tongue darted out to wet her bottom lip while she listened to me.

My cock hardens instantly. I grip the base. It literally throbs in my fist. Without thinking, I spit into my hand and start working myself over, twisting at the crown where I'm most sensitive. Pre-come immediately beads at the slit, slick and warm as I smear it down my shaft.

I imagine her mouth there instead of my fist. Dark eyes looking up at me, lips straining around the girth of my cock. My strokes quicken. Pressure builds at the base of my spine. I'm close now, hips lifting off the mattress, muscles tightening.

When I come, it's a full-blown explosion. Hot, sticky ropes spatter across my stomach and chest and hit the underside of my chin. I lie there panting, cock still twitching in my grip, fluid cooling on my skin.

The moka pot hisses from the kitchen, snapping me out of the orgasmic haze. I drag myself up, wiping my stomach and chest off with the edge of the sheet. My cock is still half-hard and heavy between my legs but I pad naked across the polished floors of my flat, leaving the dirtied sheets behind.

The strong, bitter coffee grounds me for a moment. I drink standing by the window, letting the caffeine fuel my body.

I have the most important meeting of my life this morning, but all I can think about is tomorrow, seeing Rosa and making her more than just a fantasy.

Dragging myself to the shower, I cup myself to keep my dick from bouncing on my stomach. When I step in, the spray hits my shoulders as steam rises around me. I close my eyes and she's there again. Kneeling before me. Looking up through wet lashes. Pouty lips open in anticipation.

I'm instantly hard. For the second time this morning, I wrap my hand around myself. Closing my eyes, I imagine her lips parting. Taking the tip at first. Swirling her tongue along my sensitive ridge.

My head falls back against the tile as I stroke faster, picturing her taking me deeper, her small hand cupping my balls, rolling them gently between her fingers. The pressure builds and I ejaculate on the shower wall in thick streams. Then stand trembling, watching the evidence spiral down the drain.

My God, control has never felt so fragile as when I think of her.

I step out of the shower, still shaking from coming twice in the span of an hour, something I haven't done in forever. My cock is hypersensitive as I towel off, but at least it completely calms down.

Satiated for the time being, I put my suit on like armor. Blue, crisp, a reminder of the man I've been for too long. Controlled. Disciplined. Never one to let my libido derail my day.

I text my older brother, Miguel, the lawyer who's made this all possible to find he's already waiting for me outside the building.

"Ready to be rich, *hermanito*?" he asks from the open window.

"Ready to be free," I correct, squeezing his shoulder as I slide in beside him.

We drive through Barcelona's morning light, as Miguel reviews the final contract points with me one last time. His voice is a comfortable backdrop to the familiar view of Sagrada Familia.

"You built something extraordinary," he adds when he's satisfied I'm prepared. "Papá would have been proud."

The meeting unfolds in the corner office of Vitis Global. Their CEO, Adriana Marquez, rises when I enter. "Santiago," she smiles as she extends her hand, "I'm proud to own the company built by a man who taught half of America's sommeliers how to actually taste wine."

I sign my name to each page as Miguel indicates. Ten years of rebuilding my training academy, flying to every wine region in the world, tasting and teaching and hundreds of sleepless nights are distilled into a few strokes.

"Congratulations" Adriana takes the wire instructions from me. "The money should clear by noon."

It's official. Within two hours, I'll have more zeros in my bank account than I ever imagined. "Thank you, Adriana. I'm honored you'll continue my legacy."

Outside, Miguel catches my elbow before I can escape. "Dinner tonight? Mamá's expecting us."

"Wouldn't miss it," I promise, embracing him properly. "Thank you, Miguel. For everything."

Back at my flat, I hang my jacket carefully because habits of precision die hard. Then I loosen my tie and stand at the window. Barcelona swells with light below me and, for the first time in a decade, I have nowhere I need to be except exactly where I want to go.

The thrill of anticipation courses through me, a constant reminder of what's hopefully to come with Rosa. We may have only had a few hours together, but something deep inside knows our connection is real. I crave her touch.

Closing my eyes, I imagine her standing before me. Hips pressed against the counter, breath quickening when I reach for her. I picture her turning her head and whispering my name. My kitchen filling with soft sounds and shallow breaths.

Every part of me tenses with desire. I fight the urge to shove my pants down and take myself in hand for the third time today.

Instead, I grab a notebook and start to write. Not work stuff. Or poetry.

A plan. For Rosa. For us.

It doesn't take long for me to fill the pages with a list of places where passion and privacy collide.

A day trip to a secluded beach, where the air is filled with the scent of salt and sunscreen. A picnic in a hidden cove, fresh fruit and cold wine shared between kisses. A drive to a quiet vineyard, where the wind rustles the leaves and the vines speak of enduring passion. An evening back in the city at a quiet table in a dimly lit corner, where we can share secrets, hopes, and desires.

If things go well, a cozy inn nestled in the hills, where the sheets are crisp and the air is cool. Somewhere I can explore every inch of her body without interruption. I'll watch her face flush with desire as she experiences pleasure like never before and revel in the moments when she lets go of all control.

The page fills with dreams. Promises. Each one, I intend to keep.

I'm finished by the time the city shifts into early evening. Standing on the balcony, I watch people fill the streets as the breeze cools my heated skin.

It's not even a question. I want to be the man who makes her every moment count. Who doesn't rush something worth savoring.

Somewhere down below my flat, Rosa is finding her way on her own. Hair loose. Eyes sparkling with curiosity and desire. Maybe even looking up at the same sky, as excited to see me as I am to see her.

Tomorrow can't come fast enough.

If I'm lucky, she'll be game for a month of exploration, discovery, and unbridled passion.

Chapter Seven

The Next Day

I'VE BEEN WATCHING THE green door for two nights.

Waiting. Anticipating.

Tonight I finally walk through it.

Can Cisa is perfection. A true locals' joint. The walls are stacked with colorful bottles, every label softened by time. A handful of tables fill an ancient, narrow room. Candles reflect off glass. Everywhere, faces are lit with the kind of warmth and joy the very best wine brings.

I'm shocked when the host greets me by name and leads me to a small table by the window. Outside, the narrow street flickers with storefronts closing for the night. I watch the strangers moving back and forth through the glass.

Each one not him.

God, what if he changes his mind?

It's happened before, so I'm not sure why I expect more from a man I met on a plane.

I'm early though, so rather than bailing out of fear, I sit, trace the rim of my wine glass and try to breathe normally.

Then I see him and my heart nearly stops.

Santiago. He moves with a grace born from confidence, not arrogance.

Holy shit, he's more gorgeous than I remember. Dark eyes. A strong jaw. Mouth made for sin and sincerity in equal measure. Tonight, he wears a white shirt with an open collar and sleeves rolled to his elbows tucked into dark trousers. Tall, lean. *Delectable.*

The faintest smile plays on his lips when he spots me when he walks through the door. It's no exaggeration—every eye in the room snaps to catch a glimpse of him.

He doesn't even notice because *his* eyes are on me.

"You beat me." He sits and scoots his chair close.

"I didn't want to be late." I shrug.

Santiago laughs. "I like a punctual woman."

With a subtle gesture, he signals the waiter and orders in Spanish without opening the menu. His voice is quiet, sure. I find myself relaxing. It's nice to let someone else decide a meal for once.

When the server leaves, he leans back. "You look rested."

"I slept for nearly a day straight," I admit. "Then walked my ass off. Got lost twice. Ate everything in sight."

His eyes spark. "That sounds like the perfect way to conquer jet lag."

"It was. Even better, it's the first time in months I woke up without a list of problems waiting."

"I've been there." He rests his chin on his palm. "You forget how to breathe until someone forces you to stop."

"You sound like you know from experience."

"I do." He folds his hands. "For the record, the rea-son I had to leave you so abruptly at the airport is because I sold my company yesterday. Ten years of work signed away in an hour. Today, I'm a free man with a nice little nest egg."

"Wow. How do you feel?"

"Strange. Excited for what's next." He hesitates. "I've been looking forward to tonight since we parted ways."

The blush from my cheeks creeps down to my chest. "Me too."

Food arriving interrupts us for a moment. I'm delighted. Garlic prawns. Octopus croquetas. Thin slices of *jamón*. A basket of bread already glistening from a vintage olive oil he recognized when he ordered.

He chose with care, matching textures and pace, the way a talented sommelier pairs courses with a story. Somehow, he anticipated everything I would have ordered myself.

He pours the wine. "Montsant. I think you'll like the balance, it's not too sweet."

"Are you guessing what my palate is?" I smile.

"I'm not...exactly." His eyes meet mine. "It's time for a confession. When I sat down next to you, I recognized you immediately because I've eaten at your restaurant. A few times. Not enough. I'd have visited more if my travel schedule hadn't been so full."

I'm immediately unnerved. I didn't expect this. At all. I can't believe I didn't notice someone like him, especially with his Spanish accent. What else have I missed over the years.

Oh, *shit*...

My hand stills on the glass. I'm an idiot. This dinner is less about romance and all about business.

Disappointment washes over me and I can't hide it. "You've been to my restaurant? Why wouldn't you have just said something?"

"Well, I was planning on it but I enjoyed our time too much." He leans back and looks me directly in the eye. "As to your restaurant, I never stop thinking about it. I love everything you're doing there."

Confusion washes over me. "My food?"

"Well, yes, and your pairings, which are brilliant by the way." He smiles broadly. "Now, it's more about the woman behind it all."

I stare at him, stunned by his blunt proclamation. My mind whirls about why I'm here tonight. "It still doesn't explain why you wouldn't have said anything on the plane."

"At first, I didn't want to make you self-conscious." He smiles cautiously. "I was fan-boying because you're brilliant. Then, it was like something washed over us and we'd known each other for years. I feel stupid for not fessing up."

His words strike somewhere deep. No comment by a critic or article in a food blog has ever felt so important.

"Well, if you've been to the restaurant, you must understand why I'm so burned out." I let out a deep breath and try to reset my expectations for the evening. As far as I can tell, he wants to be friends. Nothing more. "I've gone for many years without a break. My parents and sister forced me to go on vacation. I didn't want to, but they mean well. I forgot how much I love being here."

"You sound grateful."

"I am. Mostly," I acknowledge, possibly for the first time. "Admittedly, it was nice for someone to make a decision for me. It's not often I have such a luxury."

His gaze softens, thoughtful. "I can work with that."

"Work with what?" I laugh. "Are you gonna plan my vacation now?"

"Maybe. If you'll let me." Santiago reaches over and takes my hand.

Well, then.

"I'm not great at letting people I don't know take over."

He leans closer. "Try it. You might surprise yourself."

The air between us pulls taut, every sound around us thins until it's merely low music and our uneven breathing.

A server appears, breaking the spell for a beat, refilling our glasses. When she slips away, Santiago's gaze returns to mine, steady, curious, too intimate for a public room.

He traces the rim of his glass. "Tell me something. What keeps you going at such a pace?"

"Creating something perfect for strangers. Watching them close their eyes when the flavor lands. It's usually the only time my head goes quiet." I take a sip of the wine. "It's the only time I stop thinking."

"You deserve to stop thinking more often for more pleasurable reasons." Santiago's accent is like warm chocolate.

"God, tell me how," I mutter and then flush from head to toe, realizing what he means.

Holy shit. He *is* interested in me.

The question is, can I handle him?

Santiago's eyes darken. "You make a decision to let go. One night at a time."

"Oh, yeah?" My stomach flips and my words come out a bit sarcastically. "Starting now, I suppose. With you?"

He tilts his head, eyes boring into mine. "Absolutely. If you want to."

God, I *do*.

More than I should. I'm not sure how, though. It's not in my nature.

Perhaps sensing my discomfort, he eases back. We finish the wine and our conversation shifts away from innuendo and invitation.

Just like we did on the flight, he and I discuss every-thing and nothing effortlessly. Every now and then our fingers graze and each time, the air thickens a little more. When the staff starts placing chairs on top of tables, he signals for the check and slides his card to the server before I can offer to pay my share.

Outside, the street glows copper under the lamps. I start to thank him for a wonderful evening, but he steps close enough for me to feel his breath. "Let's not let tonight end here."

"Okay."

His mouth meets mine. Firm, certain, tasting of wine and the promise of more. The kiss builds, slow, un-hurried, until I forget every reason to hesitate. When we finally pull apart, my heart is pounding so hard I'm sure it's visible.

"Tell me to stop." He rests his forehead on mine.

I don't.

In fact, I clutch his shirt so he can't step back.

I angle my face up, lips finding his again, slower this time, deeper, until thought gives way to sensation. His hand slips into my hair, the other steady at my waist, pulling me closer. My body presses into his, soft meeting solid, and the world narrows to heat, breath, and the sound of his low exhale when I open fully to him.

I kiss him harder, hoping he understands what I can't yet say.

My body explains what I want.

When we eventually break for air, I find my voice.

"Would you like to come to my place?"

Chapter Eight

SANTIAGO

SHE UNLOCKS THE DOOR and gestures for me to step inside. Her rental is simple. One couch, a small flat-screen television connected to a small kitchen. Tall windows overlook the narrow street below. A short hallway leads back to the bedroom, I'm guessing and probably the bathroom. There's a loaf of bread on the counter next to a few bottles of wine lined up like plans she hasn't made yet.

"My home for the month." She sets her key down on the counter. "It's cute enough."

"Nothing wrong with a safe place to sleep." I wink.

Her laugh comes out low, surprised. She reaches for a bottle. "Wine?"

"Only if we give it room to breathe." I reach for the corkscrew.

She glances at me, amused, and nods. "Spoken like a true expert."

"Well," I smirk, unashamed, "you opened the door for it."

We dig through the cupboards, find a decanter and I pour it carefully, watching the dark red swirl and settle. Our silence stretches, easy but charged. I want to kiss her again, but I resist.

For now.

She's breathtaking. Barefoot. Hair loose from its knot, a few strands brushing her collarbone. Her lips are flushed from the wine and our kisses. The thin strap of her black dress slides off one shoulder, exposing a hint of freckled skin.

She isn't posing. Or trying too hard. Rosa is a *real* woman.

It's hard to stop staring.

"Give it ten minutes." I manage to set the wine bottle down.

"Ten minutes, huh," she repeats, half-teasing. "You're *very* precise."

I tuck a lock of hair behind her ear. "Habit of the trade."

Rosa blushes and looks down, her hand hovering near the decanter as if searching for something to do.

I reach for it first, along with two glasses. "Come on." I nod toward the couch. "Let's be comfortable."

She hesitates, follows me over. I set everything down on the coffee table. We sit close, not touching. The cushions dip toward the center where our knees nearly meet. She folds one leg beneath herself, hem of her dress brushing her knee.

Funny, for all my self-control, my pulse doesn't care about patience.

Rosa glances toward the decanter. "So this is what we do while we wait? Stare at the wine?"

"We talk." I lean toward her. "Or pretend not to think about kissing again."

Her mouth curves. "Maybe both."

I shake my head. "You surprise me, Rosa Delgado."

"Good. I like surprising people who think they've figured me out."

I watch her, the playfulness in her voice catching somewhere deep. "I didn't expect you to be..."

She tips her head, cautious. "What?"

"Funny. Self-depreciating. Gorgeous. Someone I can't stop thinking about."

Doubt flickers in her eyes. "You're not *seriously* trying to flatter me."

I shake my head. "No, of course not."

"*Uhh*." She exhales, half laugh, half warning. "You barely *know* me, Santiago."

"I know what happens to my heart when I look at you," I admit quietly. "I haven't been able to stop reliving every moment of our flight."

She hides her face behind her hand. "You're trouble."

"Probably." I take her hand and move it away. "Maybe the *good* kind?"

Her laughter fills the small room, rich and unguarded. When it fades, she studies me. "How old are you, anyway, if you don't mind me asking?"

"Forty-five," I say. "And you?"

"Thirty-three." She swirls the decanter absently. "You've achieved a lot at such a young age. You seem to have balance. My sister says I work too much to have a life. She might be right."

"If I remember from our plane conversation, she's the one who just got married?"

She nods. "Marcella. She's a lawyer and used to be a workaholic. Until she met her husband, Seamus. He's a surgeon, eight years younger. Now she's full of advice about balance between love and work."

I lift an eyebrow. "You sound unconvinced."

"She means well." Rosa fiddles with the hem of her dress. "I don't have a point of reference. I've never had a serious relationship, unfortunately. A few attempts. Turns out, I'm usually terrible at reading the situation."

I shake my head. "I bet if you thought about it, your gut knew. I find it hard to believe your instincts are so off. You read flavor better than anyone I've ever known."

"It's not the same."

"It's close," I insist. "It's mostly about trusting yourself and your instincts."

She hesitates. "I guess you have a point. For me it's easier with food. I *know* what to do with food. With people? Not so much."

"Anyone would be lucky to be with you, Rosa."

Her eyes flick to mine, uncertain. "Well, thank you. I haven't...done *this* in a while."

"What's a while?"

Her lips press together. "Ummm. Embarrassingly, years."

I nod slowly, absorbing, not startled so much as honored she's willing to be honest with me. Now I know how important it is for me to be careful with her.

She watches me intently. "You think it's strange."

"No, It makes sense. You've been focused on other things. I was actually thinking all the better for me." I squeeze her fingers and let go, reaching for the decanter. The wine should be ready.

I pour us each a generous glass and hand her one. Her fingers brush mine. Tentatively. We clink.

"What are we toasting to?" she asks.

"To instincts worth following."

She holds my eyes as we drink. The wine is deep, alive. Exquisite.

Rosa swirls the liquid in her glass. "So, what about you? Any girlfriends since your divorce?"

"None. As for the rest...it's been well over a year." I lean back on the couch. "I filled the void with strangers for a while. It didn't take long to realize meaningless sex was emptier than being alone."

"And now?"

"Now I'm here, with you. I can't explain it other than to say you've reawakened something dormant."

My straightforward words hang between us. I'm shooting my shot. The ball's in her court.

Finally, she laughs nervously. "You talk like a man who's pretty self-aware. You seem to know what you want."

"I do." I take a long sip.

"What?"

"*You.*"

She looks away, then back. "Once again, I find it hard to believe. You don't know me."

"Rosa, trust me. I know enough." I hold her gaze. "You carry the world on your shoulders and pretend it doesn't hurt. You think control keeps you safe when it's making you tired. You'll do anything for the few people you allow into your life. I also think you're lonely, hiding behind work. I know this because I'm the same."

Her breath catches.

"You're here for a month, right? Let's take a chance on each other and spend it together. Neither of us has anyone relying on us. Let me show you Spain. It would be my honor. Best of all, you won't have to plan a thing. I already have a ton of ideas."

She bites her lip. "I wasn't looking for a tour guide."

"I'm not offering to be your tour guide. I'd like to see if this thing between us is what I think it is. Let's indulge. Wine. Food. Romance. Whatever you're up for."

The air changes. Her pulse jumps in her throat, visible in the dim light.

"You're serious?" she whispers, as if the thought of hanging out with me is incomprehensible.

"Completely."

Something in her breaks free. Fear or hunger, I can't tell. She moves first, quick and impulsive, kissing me before I can finish the thought. Then suddenly she's grabbing at my cock through my pants, her grip awkward and too tight.

I cover her hand, steady, not stopping her but also making sure she understands I don't expect this from her. "Easy, Rosa. This isn't about me tonight. I want it to be about *you*."

She looks at me almost in awe. Like she's never heard of such a thing.

"I want to give you a chance." Her voice catches.

I search her eyes. "Good. Shall we head to your bedroom?"

"Yes." She nods, a small but monumental gesture.

I rise and offer my hand. Her fingers slide into mine and immediately something shifts in the air between us.

With absolute certainty, I know nothing will be the same after tonight.

Chapter Nine

SANTIAGO LEADS ME DOWN the hall, his hand firm around mine.

My heart won't slow.

In my experience, sex has always been the guy taking what he can get and leaving me high and dry. Time and time again. For the past few years, hooking up hasn't been a priority. Not when I can take care of myself better than any man ever could.

Until now, maybe?

The bedroom comes into view. My skin tingles and the ache between my thighs is sharp. I'm soaking wet from anticipation.

God, I hope he'll show me what I've been missing.

He turns to me, fingers brushing my jaw. "Breathe."

I do. Barely. Then he pulls me closer and I stop thinking altogether.

By the time he kicks the bedroom door shut behind us, I'm drunk on him.

His fresh, clean scent. His velvety voice. The molten weight of his stare.

He lifts me and I wrap my legs around him with desperation. I don't have time to be inhibited, I want whatever he'll give me. Santiago pauses at the edge of the bed, then places me down and stands over me in a storm of stillness. Towering, composed, yet seething with a sexual tension crackling beneath his skin.

His gaze flicks over my body, tracing the curves and hollows like a map he's destined to follow. Worship isn't the correct word. It's something older. Deeper.

Surrender.

No, *ceremony*.

"Still sure?" It's not just a question. It's a warning. A vow.

I can't breathe, but I nod anyway. "Yes."

He moves toward me with patience, each step a slow obliteration of space. My throat pulses wildly in time with my heartbeat. His fingers slide up the side of my face. Featherlight and reverent, sparking electric shivers as they pass over my skin.

When his mouth brushes my temple, it detonates something in my spine. "Tell me if I move too fast."

"Not fast enough." I bite down on my lip.

His grin is dangerous. "God, you're perfect."

Our next kiss is not soft. It's a collision of mouths and intent. Wild and exquisite. Teeth grazing lips, tongues flicking and retreating, then diving again. I pull him into me, fingers threaded into the thick silk of his hair, tugging until he groans into my mouth.

Time bends and breaks. The world outside ceases to exist.

When Santiago's hands ghost down my arms, I shudder like a tuning fork. He waits, his control stretched tight, as I lift my arms so he can pull my dress over my head. He tosses it to the floor, leaving me naked except for a slip of lace and nothing else.

"You're…" He swallows hard, voice gone rough. "You're the most fucking beautiful thing I've ever seen."

I flinch out of reflex, years of deflection rising like armor. "Stop."

"No." His voice is a command. "You don't get to look like that and not know how stunning you are."

Then he's on me, mouth on my throat, dragging his tongue across the soft skin until I cry out, hips arching into him. His hands find my waist, my ribs, my ass with a desperation I've never experienced. He's learning me. Worshipping me.

With clumsy fingers, I reach for his shirt and undo it, one button at a time. Santiago's chest is a study in heat and sinew. Muscle carved beneath bronze skin. My palm runs down his sternum and he trembles under it. When the last button opens, he shrugs out of the shirt.

I swear, the sight of him bare makes my lungs seize.

He lowers me back into the bed, mouth moving with determination. Down my neck, across my collarbone, to the swell of my breast. When he sucks a nipple into his mouth, his tongue lashes rhythmically. The friction detonates pleasure straight to my pussy. My fingers claw at the sheets, thighs pressed together aching for something to fill the void in between them.

"Holy fuck, you're astonishing," Santiago moans into my skin. "God, Rosa, I've got to feel how wet you are for me."

His hand cups me through the flimsy lace. Then he peels my panties down in a single, fluid motion, like he's unwrapping something too precious to tear.

Seconds later, his fingers slide over my slick heat, stroking my clit in torturous circles. Building. Breaking and building again. My back bows as I utter a sound-less gasp.

He watches my reaction, eyes molten, lips parted like he's praying.

When he decisively slips two fingers inside me, he curls them just so and my vision stutters. It's not just penetration, it's possession. He finds my secret place and drags over it again. And again. My legs shake. My whimpers are loud, uncontrolled.

"Right there," he growls when he hits me just so. "I've found it."

I fist the sheets, teeth clenched, breath ragged as he strokes the spot over and over. When I'm about to tip—

He stops.

I nearly sob with frustration. *"Santiago—"*

"If you're okay with it, I'd like to be inside you. The first time I make you come, I want to feel you squeeze my cock." He kneels between my thighs and yanks his boxer briefs down and off. His impressive shaft is flush on his belly. He strokes himself once, twice, eyes locked on mine, before guiding the head to my entrance.

"I can't come this way," I sadly admit, trying to close my legs.

"Rosa." Santiago breathes and presses my legs apart with his knees. "I promise. Tonight is the final night you'll ever be able to say such a horrible thing. I'll make sure of it."

His cock hovers, the tip scarcely breaching my entrance while he waits for permission.

God, I want him to be right. Before I can reconsider, I nod once.

He sinks in slow, inch by maddening inch, until he's buried to the hilt, his hips flush with mine.

Despite how wet I am, the stretch is hot, thick, overwhelming. A burn melting into bliss. For a breathless moment, he holds himself there, eyes locked on mine as I adjust to his size.

When my pussy relaxes, he draws back and thrusts deep. Once. Twice. By the third pass, we begin to move in a rhythm older than language. His hips grind into mine. I rise to meet every pulse. His hand tangles in my hair, the other grips my thigh to anchor me in place. Our bodies slap wet and frantic, sweat-slick and shimmering in the dark. My nails dig into his back. Groaning. Panting.

"Your body is made for sin," he grits. "I'm gonna worship every fucking inch of you."

My climax hits me without warning and crests like a wave. Unforgiving, immense. It slams through my body into my core, which locks around him.

Every muscle taut. Every nerve electric.

I cry out, raw and holy. If this is what it means to be claimed.

I'm all in.

We collapse together in a slow, gasping tangle. His weight presses me into the mattress, arms quaking as he braces himself above me.

Neither of us speaks at first. Words seem irrelevant. Too small for what we experienced.

He shifts gently, pulling out as he trails a kiss down the side of my neck. When he lays next to me, I'm surprised when his rigid cock burrows into my hip.

At first I'm impressed by his stamina.

Then it occurs to me, we didn't use a condom and nothing's leaking out of me.

He hasn't come yet. He didn't let himself because we didn't use protection. The realization strikes like a spark in the fog of my afterglow.

"Rosa…" Santiago presses his forehead to my temple, voice rough with restraint. "I got caught up. I wasn't… I didn't anticipate we'd get here so fast," he breathes, searching my face. "I didn't bring anything. I wasn't planning to *fuck*. I'm so sorry I didn't stop before…"

I blink up at him, my body still molten, nerves singing. "I didn't expect this to happen either, but it isn't your fault. We're both consenting adults. Unless you give me reason to think otherwise, I don't regret it."

He exhales, with relief. "I was selfish. I can take care of you so many other ways. We should have discussed this…before. If it alleviates any worry, I was honest when I told you I haven't been with anyone in over a year. I'm clean. I've been tested. I would never deliberately harm you."

His earnest, unpolished words sink into me.

I hear the question inside the confession. I sense the hesitation. His desire warring with the fear of crossing a line with me.

Something uncoils deep in my belly, and the answer comes not from logic, but from the raw place he seems to touch "I want to make you come too." My voice trembles with truth. "Inside me."

His eyes widen, not with lust. Something deeper.

"Are you sure?" His hand slides along my jaw, cupping it like I might vanish. "We don't have to—"

"I *want* to." I cover his hand with mine. "Obviously, I'm clean too. I'm also protected. I have an IUD. I want this. I want *you.*"

Santiago groans softly, like the sound has been torn from him. "Fuck, Rosa..."

Then he kisses me again. Messy and consuming as he shifts his hips and guides himself back to my entrance. The slick, blunt head of his cock presses into my opening. This time, there's nothing between us. No questions. No barriers.

Only heat and trust.

He pushes in and the sensation the second time around is *devastating*.

My body stretches to take him, the fullness stealing my breath. It's raw and overwhelming and *right*.

I moan into his mouth and wrap my legs around his waist as he sinks deep and *deeper*, until I'm utterly filled.

"Oh my God." I throw my head back. "You're the key I was missing."

He holds still, buried to the hilt, chest heaving against mine.

"Ahhhh, yesss," he rasps. "I won't last, you're too much like heaven."

"Don't hold back." I kiss the corner of his mouth. "I want you to fill me."

His eyes widen and lock on to mine. Something shifts—lust, yes, but also something more feral. Primal.

Me giving him permission flips a switch inside him.

Santiago grinds deeper and faster with every thrust. His hips rotate and swivel to ensure the head of his cock zeroes in on the sensitive parts of me still swollen and fluttering from my previous orgasm. Our rhythm builds. My hips rise to meet him as I chase the edge again.

This time, the burn begins low in my belly, coiling tighter and tighter.

His tempo turns desperate, erratic.

"I'm so fucking close," he growls. "God, Rosa, I'm gonna lose it…"

"Yes," I moan, clinging to him. "I want it. I want *all* of it."

With a broken cry, he drives deep one final time, his whole body tensing as he spills everything he has into me. Thick, hot, and endless. The flood of his release trickles down my inner thighs and the sensation of every throb and pulse of his cock trembling through the aftershocks nearly wrecks me.

Our intimacy ignites a fuse I didn't know was waiting to be lit.

My second orgasm rips through me, raw and liquid. My body clamps around him, milking him. Waves and waves of the most exquisite pleasure ripple through my core. When the spasms fade, he doesn't pull out. He stays pressed inside, his forehead buried in the curve of my neck.

I lie there, trembling, filled with his weight, his heat, his come.

And I *love* it.

I love the *mess* of it, the *claiming*. The way my body has been stretched and used and is now gloriously *his*. I *want* more. There's no going back.

He shifts slightly, drawing lazy shapes on my hip with his thumb. "You okay?"

"I've never felt more okay." A small smile curls at the corner of my lips.

Santiago kisses my temple, his lips soft and reverent. "Even if we didn't mean for us to go this fast," he murmurs. "I don't want to stop."

Neither do I.

But I don't say it. Not yet.

Instead, the world narrows to a tangle of heat and heart, bodies trembling, drenched in each other. He shifts, careful and slow, then slides out of me with a soft, aching drag. The bed sighs beneath us as he pulls me against him, his chest to my back, one arm looping tightly around my waist.

His cock, still half-hard, nestles into the curve of my ass, sticky and warm, and somehow this lingering contact is more intimate than anything else we've done tonight.

His lips find the top of my head. I let my eyes flutter closed, muscles slack with surrender. He holds me in place, hand splayed across my belly like he's trying to memorize the shape of me from the inside out.

He strokes a lazy pattern just beneath my navel, then lets his hand drift lower until his fingers move gently over my still-sensitive clit, each touch light but devastating, like he's trying to tease another tremor out of me just to prove he can.

A whimper escapes, small and helpless. *"Santiago..."*

"Let me," he whispers into my skin. "I want to make you come again. Slowly this time."

Within a few minutes, he's fully erect, nudging at my entrance, his fingers still stroking as he presses into me with aching care, inch by inch we're fully merged.

He doesn't thrust. Or chase a climax of his own.

His fingers work me, slow and devastating, until a pleasure so acute and unyielding creeps up like dense, inescapable mist. My body clenches around him in ripples, not harsh spasms. My soft cries swallowed by his kisses.

The intensity of this orgasm is infinitely deeper, shattering everything I knew before.

After, he wraps himself tighter around me, hand at my belly, cock submerged inside me, like he belongs there.

"Do you know what's happening between us?" he whispers.

I nod, breath shaking. "I think so."

"Sex has *never* been like this for me." His voice is strained with emotion. "Making love with you is like the first time, only a million times better."

The air stills. A warm silence stretches around us. His touch softens. Fingers drift in lazy strums over my skin. Our bodies remain joined, and in the quiet of my rental bedroom, something new takes root.

Something lasting perhaps?

God, I need to get a grip. A transformational sexual encounter doesn't mean anything, really.

I need to live in the moment. Enjoy being filled, held, and whole.

Hopefully have a few more orgasms.

No need to give my heart away so soon.

This is more than enough for now.

Chapter Ten

ROSA IS WRAPPED UP in me.

Her chest rises in slow, shaken breaths. Her skin glows in the low light. A blissful look on her sleeping face roots me in place.

I haven't moved. I don't want to. I can still imagine the sensation of being inside her, every inch of her body slick and gripping and *mine*. Sex with her has snapped something into place for me. I don't care if we haven't known each other long.

We belong together. I would drown in her if she let me.

Now Rosa's body is limp and gorgeous. I shift slightly, cupping the back of her head so she stays put in my arms. In doing so, she emits a soft sound of contentment. I'm careful not to wake her, but I can't stop touching her. My thumb brushes her temple, the palm of my other hand rests on the slight swell of her belly.

Pressing a kiss into her damp hair, I attempt to steady the drumbeat in my chest. I nearly fucked everything up by forgetting to talk about protection before I thrust inside her body. Once I realized what I'd done, she was too far gone for me to put the brakes on.

She looked at me like she was giving me more than her body. Offering something I didn't ask for and didn't know I needed. I wasn't prepared for the trust she placed in me, despite our complicated romantic pasts.

I didn't want her to have another disappointment and I'm glad I didn't stop.

Because, I'll never forget Rosa's look of surprise when she came all over my cock after insisting it wasn't possible. When her eyes fluttered closed and her body locked around mine, it was heaven, even if I staved off my own release.

With the protection conversations behind us, we're free to explore each other freely. Until last night, it'd been a decade since I was inside a woman unsheathed, let alone allowed myself to come. Well worth the wait for this to happen with Rosa.

These precious moments are now forever seared into my soul and we haven't even scratched the surface of what her body's capable of.

"I want to make you come too. Inside me."

Ahhh, her words.

Rosa's right. She's the lock and I plan to be her only key.

Her *forever* key.

We've found each other. I'm surrendering to fate.

She and I are more than instinct and discovery. We're something elemental. She's burrowed under my skin, lodged between my ribs, thrumming with every beat of my heart.

The universe didn't miss; it aimed Rosa straight at me and I'm going to learn her body to draw out orgasms she's never dreamed of having. From a touch. A whisper. A lick. I'll relish every shiver, moan, and gasp.

It isn't about control. It's devotion, stripped bare and burning. She deserves to know she's safe now—*worshipped*.

Her leg shifts slightly and I look down to see a drizzle of my come trickle out of her, thick and intimate.

I'm instantly hard again. I press a kiss into her shoulder. She stirs, eyes half-lidded, but now awake.

"Hey, beautiful. Are you okay?" I squeeze her tighter to me.

She nods, breath catching. "Better than okay."

I brush her hair from her face and rest my palm over her heart. "Can I ask you something?"

She tilts her head, curious.

"I know it's been a while for you." I kiss her temple. "Since someone touched you like this. Loved you like this."

Her gaze doesn't flinch. She doesn't look away.

"Yeah. It's been a while since I've had sex." Her eyes meet mine, steady, vulnerable. "The thing is, when you said it felt like the first time, I realized we've had very different sexual history. I didn't know my body was capable of reacting like this. I had no idea I could experience this much pleasure. You've shown me what it *can* be if you're with the right person. No one's ever touched me like you. Loved me like you. As far as I'm concerned, tonight *was* my first time."

Her words knock the wind out of me. I'm a lucky man. Someone should have seen her. Showed up for her. Rosa's given *me* this opportunity and I'm not going to waste it.

I slide my palm down the curve of her belly to her clit.

Her voice is almost teasing. "Again?"

"Not for me. For you."

Her brows lift, but I see it in her eyes. A flicker of surprise. The quiet war she's still fighting, even after everything we just shared.

"I'm not finished with you, Rosa." I drag my finger through her slit. "Not until you know your body is made for decadence. Not until you stop second-guessing how desirable you are."

Her lips part. "Santi—"

I lean in, kiss her slowly. "Let me worship every part of you. Free your mind of inhibitions. I'll show you we haven't even scratched the surface."

She breathes out, shaky but sure. "Yes. Okay."

I move down the bed and gently nudge her thighs apart. Rosa opens for me again, hesitating then unflinching. Even at her most vulnerable, she's powerful.

Fuck me. She's flushed from earlier and glistening—our combined release mixed with her renewed arousal. I love seeing her filled and undone and *alive*.

I lower my head, cover her pussy with my mouth and taste her like I'm starving. She gasps, hips arching, hands flying to the sheets.

Her clit is over-sensitive, quivering, so I take my time. I want to learn her every reaction. Every shift in breath. Every subtle quake.

I don't let her hide. I kiss and lick and hum into her until she moans out loud, voice ragged, raw, *real*. When she comes, it's with an unbridled, keening moan, breaking everything open in the air around us.

Encouraged, I *drink* her, slow and deep, pushing my tongue into her like I'm trying to memorize the taste of her surrender. Of us. Her core tightens and seizes as I double and triple down. My tongue circles her clit, then softly sucks on it, coaxing another climax from her like pulling flame from coal.

Using my thumbs, I spread her wide open and drag my tongue through her most secret folds, sucking on her outer and then inner lips before focusing on her sensitive little nub again.

She yelps, hands tangled in the sheets. "Santiago—*I can't—*"

"Yes, you can." I kiss the tender skin above her wisp of dark pubic hair. "I promise."

Resuming my feast, I let my fingers join my mouth. One, then two. Slow and smooth, curving until I locate the spongy spot in her channel. I watch her eyes flutter, mouth slack, pleasure blooming across her face.

I hold her there, steady. Present. Relentless.

Rosa's next orgasm hits her like a typhoon. She sobs and punches the bed with her fists, hips jackknifing off the bed. Her cries sound possessed.

I move up her body and kiss her parted lips. "Do you want more?" I guide my cock to her entrance.

She nods, a soundless, aching yes.

I slide back inside her and everything else falls away.

We don't speak.

We don't rush.

We move in a rhythm our bodies already seem to know.

When I come, it's with a fierce stillness, buried so deep in I forget where I end and she begins.

Chapter Eleven

The Next Morning

It's midmorning when I wake up.

Light spills through the sheer curtains in golden bands, like grace.

Santiago lies beside me, his chest rising in a steady rhythm, one arm flung across my waist like his body can't stop touching me, even in sleep.

I've never experienced anything like this. Never knew it was possible. I don't want to break the magic spell.

Santiago has unlocked a piece of me aching to be set free, and there's no going back.

Last night this man gave me every inch of his focus. Eliminated my self-consciousness with every kiss, every touch, every orgasm. What happened between us was more than sex, it was something *transformational*.

Logically none of this makes sense. People meet and fuck each other silly every day. That isn't what happened. Well, we did, I guess, but it was so much more than how many times he made me come—and I've absolutely lost count.

What's going on defies logic. Every cell in my body is drawn to him spiritually, physically, and mentally. Like we're two halves of a whole and now we've found each other.

I can't explain it and, for the first time in my life, don't care to analyze it much.

I know what I know.

He's mine and now it's my turn to reciprocate.

I kiss his chest tentatively. He doesn't stir. Trailing my lips downward, I feather kisses across his collarbone and on his nipples. I move the sheet and continue down his stomach, until I see his cock. Soft, resting against his hip.

It's my first look when he's not fully erect, and even in its dormant state, impressive.

He shifts a little as I move the sheet off him completely and take him in my hand. I kiss from his crown down his shaft, eliciting a small twitch so I repeat, savoring him more with each pass.

Santiago's hips shift when I flick out my tongue and drag it up and down the thick vein along the underside. He tastes musky and salty and of something a little sweeter I can't pinpoint.

Oh. It hits me. I realize the taste is probably *me*.

This triggers a new memory of last night when he licked his own come out of my pussy. Spent what seems like hours worshipping my every nook and cranny. My core clenches as I remember the hottest thing I ever experienced in my life.

Heat rushes through me and, without thinking, my lips close over the tip of his cock. I swirl my tongue into his little slit and suck.

He groans, still sleeping, as his cock fills.

I take more and more of him into my mouth, bobbing up and down until the tip touches the back of my throat. In an almost trancelike state, I savor and suck, coating him with my saliva.

Somewhere in my haze, I hear his voice graveled with sleep and surprise. "Rosa…"

I hum around him, committed. His cock is harder now, hot and pulsing as I explore him with shallow sucks and gentle licks. As he lengthens and thickens, it's impossible for me to take him entirely in my mouth anymore so I wrap my hand around his base, hoping I'm doing everything the way he likes.

My goal is to give him as much pleasure as he gave me.

Breathing through my nose, I flatten my tongue and lick from the base to the tip, wetting him thoroughly. My cheeks hollow around the length of him. He groans and bucks into me. His hand finds my hair. Not to push, not to control, but to guide.

"Fuck, *yessss*," he grits out. "You feel amazing, baby. So fucking tight and wet."

The praise steadies me.

Subtly, he shows me what he likes with the slow rock of his hips. He doesn't force himself too deep and isn't rough, but it helps me learn how to please him. I swirl my tongue around the head again then drag it down his shaft.

He grimaces and bucks. "Will you go lower?" His thumb brushes my jaw. "Suck on my balls?"

"Like this?" I lift his cock and suck them gently, one at a time. The sound tearing from his chest makes my core tighten.

"God, Rosa..." His hips gyrate. "You're a goddamn miracle."

I smile and press his thighs apart, bolder now. Eager to make him let go so I can drink him down, I increase my pace. Licking and laving, fondling his ball sack while my tongue teases the head.

"Am I doing okay? Are you close?" I peer up at him through his spread legs.

He nods. Gently. Affectionately. Decisively.

He reaches down to cup my cheek. "I could let go but I'd rather be inside you. Come up here."

He sits up and draws me into his lap.

"Let's do it this way." He guides me to straddle him.

I blink. "You want me to be on top?"

"Yeah." His hands glide up my sides, thumbs brushing the underside of my breasts. "I want to look into your eyes and come together."

Oh. My. God. *Yes*.

I settle over him. His cock, slides between my folds. He doesn't shift to push inside, instead, he angles my hips, palms firm on each of my ass cheeks.

"Feel how hard you make me?" he purrs as he moves me against him. My clit drags along the thick ridge of him, just beneath his head. "Right there. Grind on me. Let's see how close you can get before we fuck."

I rock my hips experimentally.

The sensation is...astonishing.

His cock slides perfectly through my slit with slow, hot pressure. The friction is a different kind of intensity. The visual of his cock nestled between my pussy lips combined with the sensation on my clit is nearly too much.

"*Oh*," I whisper.

He watches me like he's in complete awe. "Yes, Rosa. Holy fuck this is hot. Do you like it?"

"God, yeah." I start grinding in slow circles, pressing down, rolling up again. His pubic bone catches me with every roll of my hips. The heat builds quickly, dizzying and sweet. My hands splay on his chest. His mouth finds my breast, and when he draws a nipple into his mouth, I cry out.

"Fuck, Santiago—"

"Keep going," he murmurs. "Take what you need. I'm yours."

He doesn't thrust. His hands remain planted on each cheek, helping me find the perfect angle as his mouth moves from my breasts to my throat and back again, devouring me like chocolate. Every time my clit drags over him, the sparks take me higher and hotter.

A wave builds, intense, consuming, *new*. I clutch at his shoulders, hips stuttering.

"Santi—something's happening—"

He looks into my eyes, breath ragged. "Let it. Let go."

He pinches my nipple hard and I detonate.

It crashes through me, sharp and bright. This isn't just an orgasm, it's so much more. My body seizes, pleasure radiating and spiraling through my center like I've been waiting to erupt this way for years. I sob into his neck, unable to stop the rush of it. My pussy trembles and clenches and then I soak him with a gush of release.

His arms are around me in an instant, holding me close.

"God, Rosa," he breathes. "You're everything."

I can barely speak. My breath comes in broken little gasps.

Santiago guides his cock inside me. The mere sensation of him stretching and filling me is so incredibly right, I come again, soaking us both even more.

He couldn't care less. He seizes my hips and fucks up into me. We move together, chests and lips fused together, faster and faster in molten frenzy. His fingers slip between us and he presses my clit with his thumb.

One little touch and I clench around him and explode yet again at the exact same time as he erupts, whispering my name like it's sacred.

After, I collapse on top of him, reaffirming this is not just sex we share. It's power. It's surrender to the inevitable.

We're meant to be together.

He leans back on the pillows, taking me with him. There's so much heat still in the air, even more of him inside me—in my body, my head, my breath.

We've slipped into a different kind of space. Not morning. Not night. A suspended reality and the knowledge our lives have changed forever.

Santiago strokes my back, his chest still rising beneath mine, slow and steady.

God, I belong here. I never want to leave this bubble.

"Come on," he murmurs into my hair. "We're a mess. Let me wash you."

He lifts me gently off him, and I whimper at the wet slide of his cock slipping free. He's right, of course, we're utterly ruined. He's dripping out of me, hot and thick. He carries me to the bathroom, arms strong beneath my thighs, turns the shower on full-force. The moment he sets me on my feet, the warm mist envelopes us.

He steps in behind me, soap already in his hands and begins to wash me like it's an act of devotion. His palms trace down my spine, across the curve of my waist and then between my legs with gentle, slow sweeps. His fingers slide carefully over every tender place, cleaning me before the water rinses it away.

My legs are weak so I lean back into him, eyes fluttering shut.

He walks us back to the tiled wall and sits on the built-in bench, spreading his legs wide. "Sit on my lap." He grips my hips to pull me down.

I turn, confused for a moment, but he tugs my hand. "Lean back on me, thighs over mine."

Lowering myself into his lap, I straddle him, facing out. The thick heat of his cock presses up between my folds. How can he already be hard for me again?

This is madness.

He slides into me with no resistance, his hands resting on my hips, holding me in place. Neither of us have any energy left so he doesn't fuck me. Or even move. We sit joined, my back against his chest, his cock buried inside me, water cascading over our skin in soft, steady sheets.

"Do you realize how perfectly we fit?" His lips brush my ear.

"Yes," I breathe. "You fill me perfectly."

His teeth graze my earlobe, and I shudder.

Then his right hand slides up, cupping one breast, fingers slick with soap. He rubs his thumb over my nipple, until it peaks under his touch. His left hand drops lower, between my legs, and he circles my clit with the gentlest pressure.

Not rushed. Not demanding.

"Santiago..." I gasp. I'm so raw I can't help but squirm.

"I want you to come again." His velvety voice cloaks me. "Let go entirely. It will *find* you. Give in to the sensations. Stay out of your head."

His words wrap around me like a spell.

He pinches my nipple gently, circles my clit. His cock roots me to him. In this position, the stretch, the pressure along my front wall is perfect. Grounding.

I clench him tightly and let go. Repeat. Lie back and allow my subtle movement to align with my breath.

"Yes, Rosa. Release for me."

There's no thrusting. No pounding. His fingers tease and coax my clit and nipple while I clench.

Like wildfire, it whooshes through me. An electric sensation from my toes up through my core. I come with a shattered gasp, breath torn from me like silk through fingers.

Santiago's arms remain banded around me. Fingers on my clit. Light pinches to my nipples. His mouth pressing kisses along my neck as I shake and shudder. This intensifies the situation as aftershock after after-shock rolls through me. I sob softly, unable to hold it in.

When the spasms finally recede a bit, I slump back, every part of me trembling. He kisses my shoulder, my neck, my jaw and then lips as his hands run up and down my soaked skin.

"Rosa," he whispers. "See? You were *made* for this. For me."

His sentiment isn't sweet. Or even romantic. It's the truth. It's like I'm reborn. His cock filling me. My body fluttering around him. Every nerve ending alive and rewired. Muscles sore in the best way.

My heart is cracked wide open. Santiago lives inside me. *With* me. Literally and figuratively.

The man was put on this planet to show me I was never meant to go without this.

I never will again.

Chapter Twelve

Two Weeks Later

SHE'S NERVOUS, I CAN tell.

She's never met the parents of a man she's seeing before. Rosa's hand rests in mine as we climb the worn stone stairs to my mother's apartment.

It's been two weeks since we spent nearly twenty-four hours lost in each other's bodies, giving each other pleasure beyond anything I'd ever imagined. In those passionate moments, our hearts twined together, changing our lives forever.

Words weren't necessary. We both knew we were hopelessly, *desperately* in love.

Then came the shower. I can't even explain it except to say it was transcendent. As we were drying off, it all spilled out of me. Against all convention, I confessed how deeply I'd fallen with her. How I wanted to spend the rest of my life with her.

She tearfully reciprocated. *"I love you more than I ever imagined possible. I never believed a man like you existed for me. I don't want to spend a moment without you ever again."*

Immediately, I asked her to abandon her rental and move into my apartment. Her eyes lifted and she agreed.

No flourish. No drama.

It's been two weeks since we moved her things to my place and I don't have one regret. She's perfect.

We're perfect.

We've wandered the cloisters of the Pedralbes Monastery in silence thick as velvet while light spilled through arches like some kind of blessing. She touched every stone as if it might remember her.

In Gràcia, she cried over a clay dish of bombas still crackling from the fryer, eyes shining as she said it made her remember why people linger at small tables long after the plates are cleared. She tasted the vermut, smiled through her tears, and told me she'd forgotten food could make her emotional.

One night in the Gothic Quarter, I brought her to a restaurant few ever find—no sign, no menu, no reservations. It opens only for those who know to ask. The chef greeted me with a nod, poured us cava from his private cellar, and left us in the courtyard while he cooked. We ate beneath wisteria, each course arriving without introduction. I adored watching her curiosity bloom into pleasure as she tasted each dish. When the plates were cleared, she leaned close and whispered, "You've ruined me for ordinary meals."

A few days later, we drove north into Priorat through vines twisting around veins of dark slate. I brought her to a small family winery I've loved for years. The owners poured from their secret barrels, smiling as they handed us glasses of deep, red wine. Rosa closed her eyes, and tasted. I watched her shoulders ease, her mouth curve, and the spark of wonder return to her expression.

Watching her fall in love again with wine and food, and the part of herself she'd buried under work for so long, is better than any vintage I've ever tasted.

The hunger for each other gets stronger with every passing day. It's always lingering under the surface, steady as breath. When it hits, we give in. We can't help it. Against warm stones in an alley, on rooftops above the city, a sailboat under the moon, between rows of vines before sunrise.

The world before her doesn't exist anymore. She's awakened a need so deep it shakes me to the core every time I touch her. Watching her open to me again and again is the purest thing I've ever been blessed to experience.

I'm powerless to resist.

Now I'm bringing her home to my family. There's no reason to wait. Rosa isn't someone I'm dating. We've skipped over unnecessary formalities.

She's it. My forever person.

As we near the door, I tighten my grip, hoping to reassure her my people will adore her.

She's gorgeous in a slate-gray linen dress we bought in town today. Her hair's twisted up and she's wearing a bit of makeup. There's such softness to her tonight, but she's not fragile. Rosa's simply free of stress and worry.

It looks terrific on her.

My mother's apartment smells like olive oil and saffron. She's been cooking all day, you can literally taste it in the air. Roasted tomato and saffron bubble in the iron of a pan she's had since before I was born. All her windows are open to the street, laundry sways across balconies. Flamenco guitar music plays on the radio.

This is my childhood and I'm proud to share it with my girl.

The door swings open before I knock. Matteo stands there, broad and composed in his usual lawyer-calm, eldest-son surety. He gives me a long, meaningful look, then turns to Rosa.

"So," he smiles as he takes her hand, "you're the woman responsible for my brother disappearing off the grid."

Rosa giggles. "I'm pretty sure he responds to texts. *Eventually.*"

Matteo holds her gaze a beat longer than strictly necessary, reading her. I watch his expression shift. Approval. Respect. Curiosity.

Good.

We move inside. My mother's in the kitchen, stirring the paella. She looks up and wipes her hands before crossing the tiled floor with arms outstretched.

"La meva nena estimada," she says in Catalan. *"Ets molt benvingut en aquesta casa."*

She kisses both of Rosa's cheeks. Rosa replies back perfectly, not showy, but fluent, and my mother's brows lift with pleased surprise.

My heart fills with joy.

Matteo's wife, Sofía, arrives with their kids, Mateo Jr., nine, and Clara, six. Sofía is sharp and elegant, her energy calm in the middle of their noise. The kids make themselves at home right away. Junior pulls Rosa toward the shelves to show her photos from his soccer season, while Clara climbs into her lap and starts weaving her fingers through Rosa's hair.

Rosa lets her. No hesitation. No discomfort.

When Sofía joins them, Rosa leans in to compliment her gold hoop earrings. A gesture so simple and sincere I watch how quickly she's pulled into Rosa's orbit.

I knew they'd love her, but Rosa fits here better than I could have imagined. Effortlessly.

We eat on the terrace with the sun setting behind us. Ma lifts her glass, eyes shining in the soft light. "To your father, Gabriel. He would have loved this day."

We all raise our glasses. The clink is small but full.

The paella sits at the center of the table, golden rice studded with shrimp and mussels, the edges crisp where the pan met the flame.

Rosa takes her first bite unhurriedly, eyes closing as she tastes. "It reminds me of my father," she says after a moment. "He used to cook on Sundays. Nothing fancy, but the house smelled like this."

Ma reaches across and touches her hand. "Then you understand. Food is love made visible."

Rosa nods, eyes soft, voice low. "Exactly."

Later, after the dishes are cleared and washed, I find myself on the balcony alone with my mother. She stands with her back to the city, the lights of Barcelona glittering behind her like a quiet truth.

"She loves you," she says without preamble.

I blink. "Yes—"

"It's written all over her. In the way she listens. In the way she looks at you when you're not speaking."

I say nothing.

Then she turns fully, eyes narrowing in the way only mothers can manage. "She's the one, isn't she?"

It's not a question.

I stare past her at the city streets I grew up on. The squares I used to play in, the hills we'll climb together one day. I see Rosa in all of it now. Her laughter in Gràcia. Her wonder in Cadaqués. Her joy stitched into every place we've touched.

"Yes," I say. "She is."

My mother doesn't smile. She steps forward and kisses my forehead like she used to when I was small.

Somehow, her acceptance of the woman I love makes it real.

Chapter Thirteen

Two Days Later

THE GREEN HILLS FOLD into each other beyond the terrace.

A bell rings from the village below, its echo winds through the vines.

I think of home, of my father who taught me to taste before I could read a recipe. I miss my parents.

My sister and my brother too. Even the restaurant, though I'm truly enjoying this time off.

On the other hand, I've never been happier. Everything moves slower here. Meals stretch, laughter lingers, flavors breathe. Santiago keeps finding ways to show me food doesn't need to impress. It needs to *mean* something.

Somewhere between these hills and his loving, I remember why I fell in love with cooking in the first place.

He left twenty minutes ago to pick up dinner from a little bodega down the road. We've had enough artfully plated tasting menus. Tonight, we both want grease and garlic. Something simple we can eat with our hands.

While I wait for him to get back, I'm curled into a chair on the terrace of our boutique hotel checking messages, a wine glass filled with cava in my hand. I haven't looked at my phone in days and when I do it's blown up with texts and voicemail.

All Marcella.

Easily fifty texts, a few threatening to fly from Seattle if I don't give her proof of life. There's a few dozen voicemails, one from about an hour ago where she threatens, "answer your phone or I will *end* you."

I grin and push FaceTime. It connects instantly.

"Okay, okay. I'm alive. Please don't call Interpol."

There's a beat of stunned silence. Then—"Holy shit. You're not in a ditch."

I can't help but laugh heartily. "Not even close."

"Where are you?" Her face fills the screen, long chestnut hair wound up in a bun.

"In wine country. Outside Barcelona."

Another beat. Then she quirks a brow. "There's a *man*."

"How do you know?" My cheeks redden.

"Uhhh...you've gone totally off-grid, your voice sounds raspy from sex and lack of sleep, and you're drinking wine somewhere rural?" She tsks me through her teeth. "Oh, there's a man."

"Fine." I shrug and take a sip of wine, unbothered. "Yes."

Marcella exhales like she's been holding her breath for days. "Tell me everything."

I don't tell her everything. Only the basics like we met in first class on the flight over. Talked for six straight hours. He asked me to meet him for wine after his business meetings, I said yes, we slept together and haven't been apart since.

By siphoning out the details, I'll admit the story sounds trite.

I don't tell her how it felt when he looked at me like I wasn't just Rosa the chef. I don't say how the minute we kissed, my body remembered something my brain hadn't caught up to yet. I don't try to explain how he touches me like I'm fragile and feral at the same time. Or the way he looks at me like he's memorizing every breath I take.

Instead, I tell her we've been traveling and how I've seen the sunrise from Tibidabo, stood in a cloister so quiet I forgot how to breathe. About the best garlic shrimp of my life. And the quaint plaza where old men drink vermut and kids kick soccer balls into fountains.

When I mention he introduced me to his family, how his mother cooked dinner and I met his brother, sister-in-law, their kids, Marcella whistles. "This isn't a fling."

I nod. "I know."

"You sound different."

I pause. "Different how?"

"Like someone opened a window in you." She looks at me moony-eyed. "I'm so happy for you."

I press my thumb to the rim of my wine glass and watch a drop of condensation slide down the side.

"You, Mom, and Dad were right. I needed to leave. I needed air."

"Damn straight you did. We were tired of watching you disappear." She looks up over her shoulder at her husband, Seamus, who waves at me from the background.

I wave back. "I didn't realize how far gone I was."

"You were a ghost, Ro." Marcella shakes her head. "Beautiful. Successful. Exhausted. You hadn't sounded like you in a long time."

"You guys booked a first-class seat like you were sending me to rehab."

"We were." She points at me. "Seems like it worked."

I laugh and recline back in my chair, holding up the phone so she can see my view. "You know what's wild?"

"What?"

"I'm...so *happy*."

Marcella doesn't speak for a beat. When she does, her voice is thick. "I've waited a long time to hear you say that."

We talk a little longer about the food, the towns, the way he looks at me like I'm a discovery he gets to keep making. She doesn't ask for explicit details, but I can hear the joy in her voice when I say things like, "He listens." Or, "He doesn't flinch when I go on a tangent about over-salting."

At the end of our call, she warns, "I know all of this seems sudden and your head hasn't caught up to your heart yet. Promise me you won't run. Don't sabotage whatever you're building because you're scared. Enjoy being in love."

"Okay." My heart beats a bit faster. "I won't."

Marcella scowls. "Knowing you, it's possible. If you do, call me. I'll set you straight."

When I hang up, the sun is sinking behind the hills, casting everything in a warm light.

I hear the crunch of gravel.

Santiago comes around the side of the terrace, holding two paper bags and an unlabeled bottle of wine. His shirt sleeves are rolled to his elbows, fore-arms tanned. His smile, when he sees me, is pure sunlight.

"You're going to be excited. They let me have the last order of anchovies." He lifts the bag. "I'm officially the best boyfriend in the world."

I step toward him before he can say another word. "I love you."

He blinks in wonder. The same expression every time I tell him the truth.

Then his voice drops, reverent. *"Rosa,"* he breathes. "I love you too."

The paper bag crinkles between us as he sets it down and pulls me into his arms. I feel his heart through his chest. Mine matches it beat for beat.

Whatever I thought love was before, this is more.

It's salt and air and time.

It's garlic on my fingers and wine on my tongue.

It's *him*.

Chapter Fourteen

A Few Days Later

Rosa writhes above me, thighs locked around my head, taste slick on my tongue.

I grip her hips and hold her pussy to my mouth like salvation. She moans, guttural and rough, fingers tangled in my hair as her body chases the third, or maybe fourth wave.

Trembling. Needy. Already wrecked and still greedy for more.

I love how free she is when we're fucking.

My hands slide up her spine as her body clenches again, a ripple of heat flooding past my lips. I groan into her. She jerks, the sound tipping her over, shaking as she comes, wild and undone. I let her grind through it, licking and sucking her slow until she whimpers, the tremble turning to sensitivity.

Only then do I ease her down and catch her when she collapses into my chest, breath sharp and shallow.

"You're going to kill me," she pants into my neck.

"You love it."

Rosa laughs, shattered and glorious.

I flip her smoothly. Her breath catches as I yank her ass into the air and press her into the cushions. Nudging her legs apart, I admire her engorged pussy, wet and ready. *Beautiful*.

I drag my cock along her slit and slam into her in one long stroke.

She gasps.

"Yes," she breathes.

Her spine arches. I grip her hair and thrust deep, watching her back flex beneath me in the afternoon light bleeding through the sheer curtains.

I reach around and twist her nipple, hard and sudden. It hits something direct inside her core and causes her to tighten around me. She cries out and then she's coming yet again.

Fuck, she's unreal in this state. I'll never get enough.

I pump faster and faster. We're loud and untethered. From the slap of our skin, to her broken moans and me shouting her name like a prayer.

Her walls clench my cock so intensely, I lose control, hips stuttering. A low growl rips from my chest as I begin to spill inside her. Instead, I pull out fast and shoot across her back, thick and hot.

She sags forward onto her forearms, panting.

I drag my fingers through my come and trace abstract designs on the canvas of her back, exploring the valleys and peaks of her spine as she shivers beneath me. Circle her pucker hinting at the pleasure yet to come.

Leaning down, I plant a gentle kiss on the nape of her neck.

"Do you trust me?" I whisper, huskily. "I want to fuck your ass."

She turns her head slightly, eyes meeting mine with a flicker of excitement in their depths. "My body is yours. I'm pretty sure you understand it better than I do."

I let my fingers linger, massaging gently. A rosy hue spreads across her cheeks, up her neck, and across her shoulders, as she buries her face deeper into the pillow.

"*Soooooo* amazing." Her voice is muffled by the pillow. "I don't know how you're going to fit there, though."

I reach for the nightstand to find the small, smooth bottle of lubricant I bought a couple of days ago. I warm it between my hands before letting it drip onto her, mixing with my release, continuing to trace soft patterns on her skin until she relaxes.

My cock is stiff as a pole again.

"I'm going to go slow, okay?" I keep my tone steady, reassuring. "Let me get you ready for me."

"Okay," she whispers, her body already yielding to my touch.

I take my time, preparing her lovingly, patiently waiting for her muscles to relax. When her breath evens out I carefully wriggle one finger into her tight ass, then another, stretching her. Coaxing her open. Then I push two fingers inside her pussy, filling her entirely, hitting her G-spot with deliberate strokes.

"Oh God," she gasps, her body trembling. "It's like...you're fucking me *everywhere*."

"You like a bit of double penetration." I kiss her shoulder.

"It's a lot," she breathes. "I'm so full, but I want more. You've gotten me used to more."

"Do you think you're ready?" I remove my fingers and guide the tip of my cock to her hole. "If you are, I'm going to replace my fingers with my cock."

"Will it hurt?" She tenses.

I pinch her clit and she spasms and relaxes. Quickly, I use the lube dripping from her body to coat my cock and flick it across her tight ass before I enter her gradually. "Not if you completely relax and let me in."

Experiencing Rosa acquiesce completely is a sensation beyond words. My primal claim making our bond unbreakable. "You're incredible," I groan. "So tight, so warm."

She turns her head, her hair a wild tangle across the pillow, "It's all you. You make me brave and free. Only you."

I move carefully, her moans and gasps guiding me, her body's responses my roadmap. I reach around to circle her swollen clit in time to my thrusts.

"Santiago," she shrieks. "You're going to make me come again."

As we rock together, the room once again fills with our shared sounds, raw and intimate.

"Go over with me," she begs. "I want your come dripping out of my ass."

Oh. Holy. Hell.

Her words trigger an orgasm so intense I nearly go blind. She follows immediately with a scream of pleasure, her ecstasy feeding mine. Tears sting my eyes, her trust in me is a heavy, precious weight. A gift I'll never take for granted.

I collapse against her, body spent, heart full.

Rosa turns and cradles my head. Her fingers reach up to brush away the tears slipping down my cheeks.

"You're crying," she whispers.

I nod, unable to speak, the emotion too raw, too real.

She pulls me closer, her body warm and safe. "I love you"." Her breath is soft on my ear. "I love everything we do together. I trust you."

"I want to marry you." My chest is still heaving. "Have a family with you. Grow old with you."

The words are a sacred truth I didn't mean to say aloud.

She stills.

I blink up at her, still wrapped in the haze, and suddenly I see the tension. Not fear. Not rejection. Something colder. Like the light dimmed behind her eyes.

She eases out from under me and reaches over to grab a drink from her water bottle.

"Rosa, are you alright? Was that too much?" Concerned, I scoot back to rest on the headboard.

"Uh, no." She bites her lip. "I—um, need to shower."

She disappears into the bathroom. The door clicks shut.

The whole room shifts. Like air pulled from a windowless space. I sit here, cock still wet, heart thumping, brain scrambled.

What the fuck just happened?

The past three weeks have been perfect. I didn't know how much I'd crave having her close, in my space, in my arms. Every single minute.

This works. *We* work.

So why does me talking about a future life together send her into retreat?

I pace the room, replaying what happened. She's given me everything. Her body, her trust, her laugh.

She lets me hold her when she dreams. Cook for her. Tease her. Bathe her.

We tell each other we love each other. Talk about places we're gonna travel to.

So how the hell did I misstep? I know I'm not mis-reading what we mean to each other.

I think of her expression. Blank, controlled, almost fragile. Not angry. Not dismissive. Distant in a way she hasn't been since we met.

Realization hits me hard, sudden and brutal.

I've pushed it too far. Pushed *her* too far.

The thought guts me.

I'm not here to pressure her. I don't need a ring. Or a title.

I need her. Full stop.

Lit up from within. Smiling in the morning and moaning at midnight.

How did I fuck it up with a single sentence?

Chapter Fifteen

THE BATHROOM DOOR CLICKS closed behind me.

I brace both hands on the counter.

My skin is flushed, breath still shallow. His come is leaking out of my pussy and my ass because I can't get enough of him. His devotion to me is intense and the reality of our situation is something I don't know how to carry.

"I want to marry you. Have a family with you. Grow old with you."

I blink at my reflection. My hair's wild. My lips are swollen. My eyes—God, my eyes don't lie. They're wide, wet, stormy. Panic has already started its climb up my throat, a low drone rising into a choke.

It wasn't a real proposal. It wasn't planned. His words were pure. True. Heartfelt.

Sincere.

He meant it. He wants to make this permanent.

I want the same thing. More than anything.

Which wrecks me more.

I don't deserve him.

I can't give him what he wants.

My diagnosis came a year ago. A routine scan after I missed a period for the fourth month in a row. I'd told myself it was stress. I was running a restaurant. Sleeping four hours a night. Burning so hard I forgot how to take care of myself.

The gynecologist was kind. Clinical, but kind.

Polycystic ovarian syndrome. Irregular cycles. Hormonal imbalance. Elevated LH. Likely anovulation. She didn't say infertile. But she said complicated. Difficult. May require intervention.

All I heard was broken.

I've not told a soul. Not Marcella. Or my mother. I couldn't bear their reaction, they were both already treating me with kid gloves. Besides, it's not like I had any prospects. What did it matter?

I shoved the folder into my closet and tried to forget. When Marcella got pregnant, I convinced myself I didn't want kids anyway. I was too busy. Too tired. Too full of ambition and responsibility with the long nights of running the restaurant and ten thousand expectations.

Tears stream down my face as the truth washes over me. In burying my own needs, I've become resentful. Short with my family and staff. Mean, at times.

No wonder my family sent me here. They didn't know why I've been so off this past year. Sending me here was their way of telling me: we want Rosa back.

God, I've wanted her back too. So much.

Now I've met Santiago.

After my diagnosis, his vision of our life together is something I gave up hope for.

It's absurd, really. I've been in Barcelona for less than a month and am hopelessly in love with a man who treats me like gold, gives me everything he has with no expectation.

Santiago has single-handedly rebuilt me and now I can't stop imagining what our children might look like.

I press a hand to my belly and try to calm the shaking in my limbs.

This isn't a first-class fling. I love him with my whole heart.

Santiago is my soulmate.

I'm terrified of losing him. Of losing this.

At the same time, I don't want him to waste time loving someone who can't give him what he wants. He's older than me, he won't want to wait. He'll want me pregnant as soon as possible.

If I let him love me, he'll build dreams on a fault line I already know will crack.

A careful knock pulls me out of the spiral. "Rosa?" He sounds hesitant. "May I come in?"

"Uh, give me a minute." I scramble for casual. "I'll be out in a second."

Silence. Then another knock.

"Please let me in."

I hesitate. Then unlock the door.

Santiago slips through the narrow gap and shuts it behind him. His expression is open and tender, though his brow furrowed like he already knows something is very wrong. He studies my face and sees something. Or maybe he detects the absence of everything I usually wear to mask it.

The two of us stand stark naked and exposed in his bathroom about to have a conversation which will burst this bubble we've been living in.

"I scared you," he says.

Immediately, I shake my head. "No. I mean...yes. But not the way you think."

"Tell me."

I bite my lip and cross my arms over my breasts. "I don't want to ruin this."

He steps closer. "What do you mean?"

"I'm not built to give you a future like the one you want." My voice fractures. "We're on borrowed time here, Santiago. I go back in one week to my life and I won't have time for long mornings or lazy afternoons or—any of this. Let alone marriage and kids."

He reaches over to brush my hair back from my cheek. "*And*?"

"And..." I look down. My chest seizes.

"There's more to it, I may not have known you long, my love, but I know you well." He strokes my chin with his thumb. "Tell me."

"I found out last year it'll be really hard for me to have children."

He stills.

I rush on. "I don't mean impossible. But close. When I found out, I was already so exhausted and I wasn't with anyone so I convinced myself I didn't want a husband or a family. So, I ignored it. Buried it. And now you're here saying things like marriage and babies and I'm—I'm unprepared for any of it. I can't be what you want. Or need."

His silence as he wipes my tears away slices me open.

When he finally speaks, his voice is so sweet it wrecks me. "You think I'm here for some dream of what could be? I'm here for *you*, Rosa. The woman who's stolen every breath I have. You're more than enough. You're it for me. If I lost you, nothing else would matter."

"No I'm not." New tears pool in my eyes. "You deserve someone who can give you *everything*."

He takes my face in his hands. "Stop this nonsense and listen to me. I want you. *All* of you. Not a fantasy. Not a child-shaped promise. You're not broken, Rosa. You're brilliant. You're wild and gorgeous and so strong it hurts to look at you sometimes."

I choke back a sob.

"My marriage fell apart because we stopped talking. We stopped touching. We let silence creep in." He presses his forehead to mine. "I won't let it happen with you. In three weeks you've become my entire world. As crazy as it is, I've never experienced love like this and never will again. I'd crawl through fire to keep this thing we're building alive."

My voice is weak. "Really?"

"One thousand percent. You're my world. Stop this madness." He kisses my nose, my cheek, my lips. "We don't have to figure it all out today. From now on, you don't have to figure it all out on your own. We tackle life together."

"I'm scared." I fall into him.

He squeezes me tightly. "I'm not. Let me ease your fear from now on."

"I love you," I sigh into his chest. "So much."

Santiago kisses the top of my head. "I love you too."

I want to believe him.

Every word sounds true.

The problem is, I've never known love at all, let alone something this intense.

I hope he doesn't crush my heart.

Chapter Sixteen

Two Days Later

Rosa's forehead rests against the window.

One arm is curled under her cheek. The other cradles a glass of wine.

The countryside slips past in streaks of green and sunburnt gold. Vineyards, silos, crooked olive trees climbing out of stubborn earth. Her hair moves slightly with the vibration of the train.

She looks peaceful. Focused. Like she's absorbing everything and committing it to memory.

I want to believe she's cataloging the view. Not the countdown.

The rhythm of the train is soft and constant.

I chose Rioja for us to spend her final few days in Spain. It's my history and has always been one of my favorite places. I love how the vineyards carve into the hills as if they have always belonged there. The wine is magnificent, holding the memory of every season of its lifecycle.

Rosa mentioned how much her father loved it here, though she never had the chance to visit while she was in culinary school. I haven't been able to stop thinking about it.

Our fathers' shared love for the region will live on in us.

He taught her to love flavor, to find meaning in every meal. Mine taught me how to discern the best grapes and find meaning in the soil.

It's partially why I've brought her here, where every-thing worth tasting begins with time and care. Maybe she'll see us and our shared family's history in the way this land endures.

At the very least, I hope she'll understand how deeply she has changed me.

Despite our little hiccup a couple days ago, we've spent the past couple days fucking, feasting, and sleeping. She laughs easily, though her eyes sometimes gaze off into the distance when she thinks I'm not watching.

I've let the days pass without further discussion because I haven't wanted to pressure her. The clock is ticking, though. Her flight is in five days. Seven until she returns to reopen the restaurant she says can't run without her.

I hope she doesn't slip back into a life she built out of fire and fear and never taking a breath and forget about me.

Shit. It's impossible for me to stay quiet another moment.

I slide my hand over her knee. "You're quiet today."

"Just watching the world go by." Her eyes flick toward me, then drop to where my hand rests.

"Thinking about home?" She nods. Barely.

I lean closer. "Can I ask you something?"

"You're going to anyway." Her lips twitch into a smile.

I squeeze her knee. "Should we discuss what happens when you leave?"

"Well." She straightens deliberately. "I go back to my life."

"To your *old* life?"

Her fingers curl around the stem of the glass. "Well, yeah. To my restaurant. Prep lists and late nights and payroll and sixty-hour weeks, I guess."

"Rosa." I study her face and witness the tension gathering behind her lashes, which is the last thing I want to see. "Is that what you want?"

"I don't know how to want anything else." She looks back out the window.

I gently cup her chin and guide her eyes toward mine. "Not true and you know it."

"No, it's not." She laughs sharply.

She picks up her wine and takes a large sip. Her hand is steady, but her chest rises and falls too fast. She's stressed. I know her tells now. I've kissed it out of her too many times to count.

"I would never ask you to give it all up," I say gently. "I'm not trying to trap you in Barcelona or chain you to my bed—though, for the record, you're welcome to stay there forever. Making you come is my favorite thing in the world."

She huffs, but I can tell by the flash in her eyes it's one of her favorite things too.

"Our discussion was intense. In my mind, we're building something real," I continue. "This is not some fling with a return date."

Her throat works around the swallow. "You're still sure you want something real with me?"

"Yes. I want you."

"That's not a plan, though."

"It's a start."

She leans back, chewing the inside of her cheek. "I don't know how this will work, Santiago. I don't know how to go home and run my restaurant and still find space for—this."

"For us."

"Yes," she says quietly. "For the version of me I've found with you."

My chest seizes with trepidation. Maybe I should have waited to have this conversation until after this trip.

"Of course I don't want this to ever end," she says. "You make me the happiest I've ever been. But I'm scared I won't survive the collision between my old life and this new one."

Ah. I get it now. "What if I stayed in Seattle close to you?"

Her eyes flicker with uncertainty.

"I can live anywhere. Most of my life has been spent traveling for work, never staying long enough to unpack. I still have a place in Seattle, though I've barely used it." I take her hand and bring it to my lips. "I want to make the Pacific Northwest my home so we can build something lasting. Not to take over, but to stand beside you, to take care of you."

The words hang between us, fragile but true.

She looks skeptical. "So, you can live anywhere in the world and you'd make Seattle home?"

"Or, Tacoma." I draw her into my side. "It doesn't matter where I live. Home is where you are."

She quirks a brow. As if I'm feeding her a line. Or maybe because the thought terrifies her.

"We don't have to solve it all today," I assure her. "You're going home soon and I need you to see a future with me. Not someday. *Now*. Not because it's easy. Because it's *right*."

She nods slowly. Then again, firmer. "I see it. It's hard for me to believe in fairytales, though. I'm scared I'll let you down."

"You won't."

"I'm scared of how much I want this." Her eyes blink up at me so sincerely relief breaks through me, flooding every corner of my being.

She's in.

I press my forehead to hers. "Me too."

She exhales, a soft sound. I take it as full surrender.

We're nearing our destination. As the train winds through vineyards, the land shifts from green slopes to dry canyons. Mountains rise like silent guardians built on patience and pride.

The land I grew up on is around the next bend. The wines hold time in them. Work done by hand. Lessons passed down generation after generation. Nothing loud, nothing rushed. Only quiet mastery.

Each time I return, the world settles into balance.

Maybe it's the harmony here, old and new, humble and elegant. Tradition still alive in every barrel.

I hope Rosa comes to believe our love can grow the same way.

Even though we're new, what we have between us carries depth. With every cell of my being, I know our love will endure if we care for it with time and heart.

My hand stays in hers.

Today is a small win, as far as I'm concerned.

For the first time in days, we're moving in the same direction.

Chapter Seventeen

Three Days Later

I WAKE TO THE weight of his hand sliding across my belly, anchoring me against his chest.

I don't open my eyes.

I don't need to.

His cock presses into my backside, already thick and hard, seeking it's home.

Santiago lifts my leg.. His mouth brushes my shoulder and my spine. A trail of heat sets my whole body on fire.

Then he enters me. Slow. Deliberate. Deep.

I exhale a sound I still have a hard time recognizing. It's not a moan.

It's surrender.

Santiago's cock moves inside me with devastating precision, each thrust stretching. Molding. Claiming. My body is now his exclusive territory. His arm locks around my waist, palm pressing on my lower belly where I can feel his thick shaft pushing along my walls from both sides. His other hand cups my breast, fingertips circling my nipple until it's a tight, aching peak.

He knows my body by heart now, teeth grazing the spot behind my ear, sending electricity down my spine. Fingers digging into the sensitive curve where my waist meets my hip. The swollen head of his cock grazes my G-spot with each thrust, making my clit throb and my vision blur.

I arch back, allowing my pussy to stretch around his thickness. As always, the initial burn has given way to slick, hot pleasure dripping down my thighs. He's so deep I swear I can taste him in my throat. His cock steadily throbs inside me.

"Tell me what you need," he murmurs.

"*You.*" Is all I can manage.

He shifts, tightens his grip on my leg, lifts it higher. The new angle hits devastatingly. My pussy clenches around him, greedy and desperate. He growls into my neck as he begins pounding into me. Each thrust harder. Balls slapping against my wet flesh with each drive forward.

"Take all of me," he rasps.

I reach back blindly, fingers digging into the taut muscle of his ass, needing something to hold on to as he fucks me senseless. His fingers find my slick clit, circling the swollen bud with perfect pressure. My pussy spasms violently around his cock as I come, juices coating him as sharp, electrifying pleasure tears through me.

He doesn't stop.

He fucks me through it until I'm boneless and gasping. Until my legs tremble and my heartbeat drowns out thought.

Then he pulls out.

Before I can catch my breath, he flips me onto my back and settles between my legs, eyes dark and full of something I can't name.

"Again," he says.

I nod, already aching for more. When we met I'd never had an orgasm during sex. Now I can't seem to stop.

Santiago presses inside once more, so achingly slow I experience every inch. He holds himself there, buried to the hilt, pulsing against my walls. His fingers tangle with mine, pinning my hands beside my head. His gaze burns deep as sweat beads on his forehead.

"I love you"." His words permeate my soul.

The deliberate restraint in his movements makes my pussy clench around him involuntarily. My breath catches as he withdraws almost completely, then pushes back in with excruciating slowness, dragging along the spot inside me that makes my vision blur.

"Please," I whimper, trying to buck my hips, desperate for more, for faster.

He doesn't give in, instead keeps his pace torturously measured. "Feel *everything*."

My body trembles beneath him, every nerve ending alive and screaming. I wrap my legs around his hips, trying to urge him deeper, but he maintains such maddening control, I want to scream. Each thrust is a slow, deep claim.

His thumb finds my clit, circling with the same un-hurried deliberation as his cock moves inside me. The dual sensation makes me scream and arch off the bed.

"That's it." He watches my face contort with plea-sure. "I'm not going to come until you let go for me again."

Pressure builds, gathering wavelike force with each languid stroke until I'm panting and begging. My nails dig into his shoulders. When it finally crashes over me, my entire body convulses. My pussy clenches rhyth-mically around him as I come harder than I ever have, which is saying a lot.

He follows seconds later with a rough sound buried in my neck, his hips finally losing that perfect control, his cock pulsing with each hot spurt.

When Santiago collapses beside me, he doesn't let me go, his arms lock around my waist as if he's afraid I might disappear.

His lips press tender kisses to my temple, my cheek, my jaw. "I love you."

The words land softly, rich with meaning I want to trust. We've spoken about Seattle, about a future, and I understand what this moment means to him.

But nothing's certain. There are no plans, no tickets, no dates marked on a calendar. Only this bed, this silence, this hope I'm scared to name.

I press my face into his neck and breathe him in. He's shown me the world he loves, and somehow, I've become part of it. I want to believe it's enough to hold us steady once I leave, but the pessimistic part of me has doubts.

Pretending belief isn't the same as proof, but it's all I've got.

However, I've never been touched, seen or loved the way Santiago does. I crave more. Part of me wants to break my whole life apart and start over from here.

I close my eyes and hold him tighter.

The reality is, I'm getting on a plane tomorrow.

This is probably the last time we'll ever be together in this way.

The best I can do is memorize everything and hope for the best.

Chapter Eighteen

Two Days Later

A MONTH AGO, ROSA was someone I admired.

I didn't know her. She's not famous in the way celebrity chefs are on red carpets or reality TV.

No, for years, Rosa Delgado's name was whispered from table to table. Her story was one chefs and sommeliers passed along in awe. A secret too wonderful to keep. A small woman in Tacoma who turned a family restaurant into something people felt down to the bone.

Intrigued, I made a point of eating there whenever I was in town. Every time, her food and wine pairings stayed with me, the flavors replaying in my mind long after the plates cleared.

Then came the fated first-class flight. Her beside me. No apron, no walls, only a quiet smile shifting everything I thought I knew about timing.

I stand in the aisle, watching her settle into her seat, unaware.

Everything in me has shifted since the day we met. The world is sharper, hungrier, alive in ways it never was before we met. I want Rosa's laughter in my mornings, her fire in my nights, her quiet in the spaces between. For the first time in my life, I'm not chasing what's next.

I'm pursuing the love of my life.

Yesterday, I let her believe I'd be two weeks behind. Kissed her goodbye. Told her I'd see her soon. My brother, Matteo, was waiting to pick up my car. I checked in, made it through security and moved through the terminal without her seeing.

Now comes the moment of truth.

When I reach our row, she's already in her seat. 2D. Hair loose around her shoulders. Same hoodie. Elbows tucked in. On the verge of tears.

Rosa's folding in on herself.

I slide into 2F.

She turns.

Her face crumples the second she sees me.

A choked sob breaks from her lips before she can stop it. Her hands fly to her mouth. I lift the divider without a word and wrap my arms around her. Her body folds into mine like we never parted.

"I told you I'd follow you," I whisper into her hair.

"You aren't supposed to be here," she cries into my chest. "You said we'd find a way but I wasn't sure..."

"I've *always* been sure."

She lets out a shaky laugh. One hand curls into my shirt. I sit back just enough to see her face. Eyes shining. Lips parted. She wants to believe this is actually happening but doesn't quite know how.

"I meant what I said," I tell her softly. "I'm yours, Rosa. Whatever that means. However long it takes. I'm moving to Seattle so we can be together. Give ourselves a real shot. You're worth it. *We're* worth it."

Her breath stutters. Her fingers trail around my heart. "*Santiago...*"

"I love you." I cup her checks with my hands. "You don't have to give anything up. Not your restaurant. Or family. Most of all not yourself."

She stares at me for a long beat, eyes wide and uncertain, weighing the risk of believing this is something real. Then she leans in and kisses me, slow, deep, deliberate.

The moment her walls finally fall, everything shifts from maybe to *meant*.

When she pulls back, her voice trembles. "Are you sure? Even if I can't give you kids? Or find out in real life I'm not the same woman you've fallen for once life gets crazy again?"

I don't flinch. Don't look away. "Even then. *Especially* then."

She tries to keep her composure, but the way she clings to me gives her away. She's in. All in.

I hold back a smile, afraid to break the spell. Nine hours in first class with me—she doesn't stand a chance.

I'll eliminate any lingering doubts.

"You've spent your whole adult life without a partner to lean on. Carrying more than anyone should. Giving everything until there's nothing left for yourself. It ends now. You have someone to lean on, if you'll let me."

The last trace of hesitation leaves her face. She slides her hand up to my jaw, thumb brushing my skin. "I don't know what comes next. I know I don't want to face it without you."

"I love you, Rosa." I kiss her temple.

She threads her fingers through mine. "I love you too, Santiago."

Outside, clouds drift across a boundless sky, but all I see is her. Rosa leaning her head on my shoulder, fingers tracing lazy zigzags over my hand.

A moment later, she exhales. It's a soft sound of acceptance. The moment she truly lets herself fall.

Four weeks may not be a long time, but for us each moment is stitched so deep, we've already shared a lifetime.

Everything from here on out is a gift we get to un-wrap together.

Epilogue - About A Year Later

THE RESTAURANT GLOWS AROUND me, alive with motion and sound.

It's Friday night, the dining room's full. Third course down without a hitch.

The kitchen steady and confident, every detail unfolding without me steering every little detail.

I can lift my head. Breathe. Enjoy the moment.

Glancing toward the wine cellar I spot him stepping out, a bottle of Viña Tondonia Gran Reserva in his hand.

Santiago glides over to a table like he's been part of this place forever. Gorgeous in a tailored black vest over a crisp white shirt with his sleeves rolled to his elbow and a wine key at his hip.

He bends to pour the wine for a retired nurse who's celebrating her 75th birthday. She clutches his arm and laughs. He answers in that honeyed Spanish I'll never get tired of hearing, then moves on to the next table, charm never dimming.

Every bottle he touches sells itself. Every pairing he suggests makes my dishes sing.

I'm not sure what makes the guests swoon more. His palate or the way he sometimes looks at me like I'm the rarest vintage in the room.

Tonight's no exception.

His eyes catch mine as he disappears behind the bar to uncork a chilled Albariño. His tongue sweeps over his lips, low and deliberate. A not-so-private promise meant for me.

Heat curls low in my stomach, spreading through me in slow waves until I nearly forget where I am. Anchored by the certainty of what it means when we're alone again.

A moment later, his hand brushes the small of my back while I pass off a ticket to Flora, our new head chef. She's better than I ever hoped. Sharp, calm, and unflappable when the fryer acts up or the rare occasion when a guest sends back some dish.

She handles the nightly heat now. My time is devoted to the creativity behind the menu.

Santiago helped me make another change to cater to what I love about cooking. Rather than an endless a-la-carte selection, we've switched to a hyper-seasonal tasting menu. Six courses. His pairings. My vision.

Tonight, the stand-outs are his citrus-slick Riesling with my charred fennel and scallop crudo and a red wine–braised short rib with his slyly chosen Syrah. Dessert seals it, a dark chocolate torte with sea salt and olive oil, matched to a late-harvest Garnacha tasting of velvet and sin.

By then, the rhythm between us is impossible to miss. A glance. A smile. A beat. A dance.

He lifts a bottle. I nod. He glances toward Table eight and I'm already crossing the room with a small plate from the pass. A bite of citrus granita to reset their palates.

An excuse to see him pour.

We speak with glances and touches. Elbows, hips, a brush to the wrist. It's the most erotic language I've ever known, except for when the doors close and the lights go out.

We're happy. Balanced. Reservations fill up months in advance. The numbers are up. The crew loves him, my family loves him, and most days I think my heart might burst trying to hold it all in.

After final service, I'm in the small pantry we converted into a wine library when the door shuts behind me.

Santiago's hands slide over my hips. "Stole you."

"You always do."

His mouth finds the side of my neck, lazy and hot. I melt. He turns me toward him, cups the place where my apron ties beneath my stomach.

"I'm dying to tell our families," he murmurs in my ear.

I press my palm over his. "Still too early."

I'm not showing. Not even close. But six tests confirmed what I already knew the second this baby was conceived.

We got married four months after the plane ride back. City hall, no fuss. His family came over for the wedding and fit in seamlessly with mine. Not one of them gave us any grief about our relationship moving too fast.

They could see we're the real deal.

Six months later, I had my IUD removed just to see if...

Within weeks, the thing we didn't dare hope for has happened.

I'm pregnant.

His thumb strokes the soft flatness below my navel. My breath shudders. He always touches me like I'm sacred.

"All of this," I cover his hand with mine, "'it's more than I ever thought I could have."

The clink of cutlery and the laugh of someone uncorking champagne floats in from the kitchen. Here, in this small room, in Santiago's arms with our child growing inside me, I've never felt more complete.

Or more whole.

Looking back at the woman who once lived for her work, I realize she never knew what living was. I learned it in Barcelona's light, in Rioja's calm, in every meal we lingered over and every night he taught me what it means to feel instead of function.

Love didn't just find me.

It transformed me.

What began as a first class fling has become my forever.

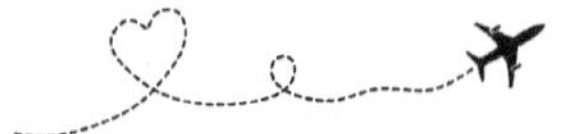

Thank you for reading *First Class Fling.*
If Rosa and Santiago swept you off your feet, I'd love it if you left a quick review: *Leave your review here.*

A red-eye flight to discovery, second chances, and a love worth the risk. *Red Eye Rendezvous* is coming in 2026. Join the Hearts Without Borders journey *here.*

Curious where Rosa first appeared? Continue reading for a sneak peek into Wistful Whispers.

Want more behind-the-scenes moments, sneak peeks, and exclusive content? Join my newsletter and never miss an update.

Behind the Scenes

I HAD SO MUCH fun writing First Class Fling because it blends two of my favorite things in the world: travel and food.

My husband and I are huge foodies. We've been to Barcelona many times and still cannot get enough. I hope I did it justice and made you feel what it's like to wander cobblestone streets, stop at tiny tapas bars hidden between centuries-old buildings, and splurge on Michelin dinners that taste like heaven and look like art.

Spain is one of our favorite places. It's so full of life and warmth, a mix of old and new, simple and extraordinary. Every time we visit, we fall in love with it all over again. The smell of garlic drifting from a kitchen window. The sound of laughter echoing through narrow alleys. The way meals turn into long conversations stretching late into the night.

Writing First Class Fling let me relive the magic in every scene.

I also wanted it to celebrate the restaurant world. My husband and I owned an Irish gastropub for 11 years, and anyone who has ever done it knows how intense it is. Long hours, endless problem-solving, and complete dedication. You give your time, your energy, and your heart to make it work.

When I started writing Rosa, it was important for me to honor the people who live this life every day. Giving her a month off in Spain felt indulgent and healing, a gift for every chef and owner who never gets to stop.

Santiago will always have my heart. He is calm, centered, and sure of himself. He already built and sold his company. He tasted success, but now he wants something deeper. He wants connection. He wants to stand beside Rosa and help her live a full, rich both in and out of the kitchen.

He's a man who does not compete with her strength, but stands in awe of it. A man who supports her completely and makes space for her dreams. Santiago is makes me swoon.

Writing First Class Fling isn't only about attraction or chemistry, it's rediscovering the soft places inside you. Finding balance, learning to slow down, and realizing how beautiful life can be when you finally make room for joy.

Most of all, First Class Fling is my love letter to Spain, to the restaurant industry, and to anyone who has ever been brave enough to take a break, breathe, and let life surprise them.

Wistful Whispers – Prologue

THE PRE-OP ROOM IS quiet.

Humming with the weight of too many emotions in too small a space.

I'm nearing the end of my third year in my neurosurgery residency at University of Washington Medical School so I've been here before.

It never gets easier.

Especially when a patient is so young and vibrant.

Miranda Black sits on the exam table, her scrawny legs swinging like a metronome of nervous energy, oblivious to the gravity of what's about to happen. She's twelve—too young to shoulder the dread etched into her parents' faces.

Instead, she looks at me with big, brown eyes, radiating a kind of trust which makes my gut twist. This little girl should have a long future ahead of her. Filled with childhood memories. Sleepovers and scraped knees, awkward kisses and graduation caps—everything she deserves but might never get.

I'd burn down the goddamn world to give her a shot at all of it.

"You ready for your big day, superstar?" I crouch slightly so we're at eye level.

She grins. "Ready as I'll ever be. Will I be able to feel it?"

"Nope." I shake my head. "You'll be asleep the whole time. When you wake up, all those nasty tumors will be gone, gone, gone."

Miranda giggles and Myra, her mom, makes a choked sound behind her. I glance up, meeting Mrs. Black's eyes. They're rimmed red. Her fingers are clenched so tightly her knuckles have gone white. Beside her, Miranda's father, Daniel, stands rigid. His face is carefully blank and his arms are crossed like they're the only thing holding him together.

How I conduct myself now is, in my opinion, the most important part of a critical case like Miranda's. Her family deserves hope. Trust. Honesty. We want to give them their daughter back. It's important to coach them through what to expect.

I gesture to Layla, the nurse practitioner. "Can you take Miranda into the children's waiting room and give her one of the iPads? We need to chat with her parents."

"Sure." Layla winks at me and leads Miranda from the room, looking over her shoulder with a distinct nod toward the exit sign.

Yeah. I've been there. Not going back for seconds.

My longtime mentor, Bryce Caldwell, clears his throat from the other side of the room, reminding me he's in charge.

"Mr. and Mrs. Black. We'll be using MRI-guided laser interstitial thermal therapy." He doesn't see the benefit of being soft—a point of contention between us on occasion. "Lasers make this surgery minimally invasive, and our goal is to remove as many of the tumors as possible while preserving healthy brain function."

Myra sucks her bottom lip over her teeth. "What are the risks, again?"

"Either way, they're severe." Bryce doesn't sugarcoat. "The tumors are deep. Near the brainstem and the motor cortex. There's a significant risk of bleeding, swelling, and neurological damage. Surgery is our best option."

"Which means there are bad options." Mr. Black chokes back a sob.

Bryce barely inclines his head. "Leaving the tumors in will make life agonizing. Along the way, Miranda will endure debilitating headaches. Seizures. All sorts of complications. There are always risks in neurosurgery. In my opinion, this operation is the *only* option."

Jesus. He's like a robot. I step in before the conversation turns completely mechanical. "We've gone over Miranda's case extensively. Dr. Caldwell is the best. I'll be assisting every step of the way." I meet their eyes, my voice steady. "We'll take care of her like she's our own."

Mrs. Black bursts into tears. "Do you promise?"

Something clenches in my chest. "I promise we'll do everything we can."

It's not the answer she wants.

It's the truth.

The OR is cold, sterile, and humming with focused energy. I feel at home here, in a room where nerves don't exist.

Where they *can't* exist.

Miranda looks impossibly tiny on the table, her head secured in a rigid frame. I've assisted in dozens of surgeries. Something about this one feels different. Maybe it's her age, maybe it's the way she looked at me before they wheeled her in here.

Maybe it's because I need this to go well—not for her. For me. For my career.

For my *sanity*.

Bryce stands at the head of the table, his presence commanding. Movements deliberate. He's been in the game forever. His reputation borders on legendary. I'd be lying if I said I wasn't grateful to be learning under him.

There's always an unspoken tension between us—the unmovable old-school mentor and the ambitious resident who embraces a new way of patient care, yet still has to prove himself.

"LITT system ready?" Bryce peers over his glasses.

"Ready," I confirm, my steady hands poised and prepared.

The MRI monitor glows, displaying the biggest tumor in real-time imaging. It's invasive, nestled dangerously close to critical structures. Not unbeatable, though.

"Target locked." I focus in. "Ready for ablation."

Bryce activates the laser. The heat burns through the tumor, destroying the cancerous tissue while sparing the surrounding brain tissue. It's delicate, precise work, and I watch every movement with fascination as I do everything he asks of me.

This man is an artist.

For the first hour, everything goes according to plan. The tumor is responding, shrinking under the guided heat. Until—

"Pressure's rising," Kendrick Lyon, the anesthesiologist warns. "Intracranial pressure is up to 25."

I glance at the monitor and panic buzzes where my breath should be. This is way too high. We've been monitoring for swelling, however, this spike is dangerous.

Lethal.

Bryce's expression doesn't change, he remains calm under pressure. "Thank you, Kendrick. We need to manage the swelling. Seamus, please adjust the laser. We need to move faster."

I nod, adjusting the fiber carefully and quickly. The pressure *has* to come down. We can't afford a rupture.

Then something shifts—something Bryce obviously doesn't see. A shadow on the monitor. Small. Unmistakable.

A blood vessel. It's too close.

I hesitate, my instinct and training screams at me to slow down. To reassess. Bryce is already moving, already increasing the intensity.

"Dr. Caldwell—" I bark.

"I see it," he snaps. "Keep going."

Except he doesn't see it. Not really. At least, I don't think he realizes...

Before I can finish my thought, it happens.

A rupture.

Blood floods into the surgical field, the dark-red liquid pooling fast.

Too fast.

"Shit," Bryce mutters. "Suction, now."

I react instinctively, grabbing the tube, working to clear the blood. It's not enough. It's not working. The pressure keeps climbing.

Miranda's brain swells despite our every effort to control it.

"We need to back off. *Now!*" I cry out urgently.

"*No,*" Bryce snarls. "We keep going."

My pulse pounds. This isn't right. We've got to do something.

The monitors blare an alarm.

"We're losing her," Kendrick croaks.

"Goddamnit. I *know,*" Bryce bites out, his hands moving fast.

It's too late.

My stomach twists. I want to push back—except I'm not the lead surgeon. I'm the resident. I assist. I follow.

Even when I don't agree.

Bryce finally makes the call. "We need to close. Now."

The weight of what's happening slams into me. I manage to keep my hands steady as we work quickly to close the incision, stabilizing Miranda as best we can.

I know the truth before we even step back.

The damage is done and the ICU is quiet in the worst way.

I sit next to her bed. Miranda is still. Machines now do the work her body no longer can. The rhythmic beep of the monitor is the only sound filling the room.

Through the window, I can see Bryce is speaking to her parents. I offered. He insisted. I don't have to hear the words to know what he's telling them.

"The surgery didn't go as planned."

"We did everything we could."

"The swelling was too severe."

"She's in a state of unresponsive wakeful-ness."

Mr. Black is frozen. Mrs. Black crumbles to the ground.

I look at little Miranda, who doesn't move. Doesn't react. Doesn't wake up.

Never will again.

I should walk away. The job is done. I can't, though. My ass stays planted, my hand clutching hers.

Could we have stopped it? If I'd spoken up sooner, would it have made a difference?

I don't know. It's too late now.

All I know is this little girl trusted me to make her better.

The sharp pull of failure settles deep in my chest.

I don't think it'll ever leave.

One moment in the OR changed everything. What he lost that day still defines him in Wistful Whispers.

Acknowledgements

Cover Design: Kate Farlow Y'all. That Graphic.

Editor: Grace Bradley Editing, LLC

Formatting: Willow Yanarella

PR: Dani Sanchez Wildfire Marketing

Literary Agent: Stephanie Phillips, SBR Media

Website Maven: Sherri Kiarsis, Ruby Moon Designs

My Right Hand: Willow Yanarella

YAY to Kaylene's Backstage Krew, my wonderful ARC Team!

Dedication

To Gareth, the man who, a year into our marriage, asked me to take a leap and open a restaurant with him.

It was our crazy idea and being part of it changed my life. Those years were filled with long days, laughter, lessons, and pride. They taught us who we are on our own and even more about who we are as a couple. We've supported each other through every professional and personal adventure, and together we've achieved more than either of us could have alone.

This one's for you.

Always.

About the Author

KAYLENE WINTER IS A best-selling author of steamy, contemporary romance.

Each character-driven novel is filled with snappy dialogue, pop-culture references and enough steam to make you fan yourself. Kaylene weaves authenticity, emotion and angst into a turbulent rollercoaster ride of love, passion and soul-searing romance always ending with a delicious HEA.

Kaylene lives in Seattle with her amazing Irish husband and her Pomsky, Phalen. She loves creating art of all kinds.

Other Titles

Find Me Everywhere

https://kaylenewinter.com/links/

www.ingramcontent.com/pod-product-compliance
Lightning Source LLC
Chambersburg PA
CBHW060449300726
48975CB00008B/2451